Founding Father

The Lost Federalist Essays of Colonel Erasmus Milton

by

Robert E. Sielschott

Bloomington, IN authorHOUSE® Milton Keynes, UK

AuthorHouse™
1663 Liberty Drive, Suite 200
Bloomington, IN 47403
www.authorhouse.com
Phone: 1-800-839-8640

AuthorHouse™ UK Ltd.
500 Avebury Boulevard
Central Milton Keynes, MK9 2BE
www.authorhouse.co.uk
Phone: 08001974150

ISBN: 1-4259-5253-4 (sc)
ISBN: 1-4259-5252-6 (dj)

Printed in the United States of America 10/25/2006

Bloomington, Indiana
This book is printed on acid-free paper.

Library of Congress Control Number: 2006908818

This book is dedicated to Elena Garza Milton and Beda Rodriguez Sielschott. The grace, goodness, kindness, and love of these two women is woven like gold thread in the tapestry of their husbands' lives. To quote my good friend, Erasmus Milton; "I find no fault in her. She is perfect."

Foreword

I must say, first of all, that this work is a novel. I am compelled to say so, for as you will see I cannot prove otherwise. I only knew my dear old friend Erasmus Milton for slightly over a year. My relationship with him at first was driven by historical curiosity, but in the end my love for the old man was more important than the obvious fame I could have garnered by leveraging the relationship as a historian. By the end of his life, I held him in such esteem that nothing could have caused me to dishonor myself by not keeping my word to him. So those items that convinced me of his valid claim as a Founding Father and brother in the "Glorious Cause" died with him, as he wished. Those proofs are no more, and nothing remains but his wonderful essays. So once again, I must say, this is a novel.

By way of explanation, let me point out that there is a Colby College, an Ohio Northern University, and of course a Columbia. There is, as well, a "Smart Room", a Matthew Sielschott, a Beda, and the rest. There is the old slave market in St. Augustine, and a Waffle House in Cleveland, Tennessee. And of course, there are the "Tacitus" essays, written by my dear beloved friend, Erasmus Milton.

You may judge his claim for yourself. To me, there is no question he has earned his desired title. He is indeed a Founding Father.

Contents

Chapter One
What a Dear Old Gentleman

I first met Erasmus Milton in June of 2004. He was an older gentleman, who carried himself with a distinguished air one doesn't often see anymore. He was tall, easily six foot, thin, tan, and healthy. In my first conversation with him, his formal manner and his mental alertness were striking. It is often said that older men pick an age at which time they decide to stay frozen in time as concerns matters of fashion, and with a man of Erasmus' age this was true to the extreme. While many times during our brief friendship he dressed in ways appropriate to a specific occasion, he most commonly dressed in the fashion of a late eighteenth century business man. His appointments were always perfect, his grey hair in a Jeffersonian pony tail (now once again fashionable), and his suits always hand tailored and expensive. He had with him the ever present cane adorned at its tip with a beautiful silver eagle.

I was walking to my car after class, having completed for the day my teaching duties at the small rural college in Ada, Ohio, Ohio Northern University. I meant only to stop briefly and ask Erasmus if he was lost. He said that he was not, and that as he himself was a lawyer he was in the process of acquainting himself with the law school. Our conversation seemed to go on and on, as if time seemed to move slowly in his presence. Before I knew it, it was evening and I was taking him home for dinner.

My wife and I spent the evening at our home in nearby Lima with Erasmus as our guest. After dinner we retired to my library, where from his vest he produced an old pipe, which he loaded and lit without asking permission. For the balance of the evening he charmed us with his presence. He was elegant, intellectually magnificent, and blatantly flirtatious with my wife Beda. My wife enjoyed this aspect of our friend Erasmus, and declared him "cute." As you will see, he was anything but.

He was living in a small village in the northwest section of Ohio called Lafayette. He was drawn to it, so he claimed, by its name, the name of "an old friend." He told me he was originally from New York, a self proclaimed "Hudson River Dandy." He claimed to have earned a law degree from King's College. Being a history professor, I found his use of this name odd, as this was the pre-revolutionary name of Columbia University. Chartered directly by King George, it was disdained as a hot bed of Tory sentiment, and later changed its name to disassociate itself with the losing side of our war for independence. Lafayette was only ten minutes from my house, and later that evening I drove Erasmus home. As he left our house, he kissed Beda's hand, told her she was an angel, and proclaimed that he had not been so smitten since the days of his youth. Beda smiled, looked at me, and said, "What a dear old gentleman."

On the short drive back to Lafayette, Erasmus Milton insisted that I visit him the next day. He said he had heard of my work, and that he wanted to share some "history of great significance" as he felt I would deal with it correctly. Not knowing what he meant, but curious nonetheless, I agreed to visit his home the next day.

Now have it known that Lafayette, Ohio, is a village in every sense. There are stout homes inhabited by stout families. There are no mansions, and no scions of wealth to inhabit them. But if a house could have such a title in little Lafayette, it was the house of Erasmus Milton. The home was a miniature version of the stately river mansions one can see overlooking any water passage in New York or New England. It has pillars in the front, a rear porch reminiscent of Washington's Mount Vernon, and a long stately drive framed by sturdy Ohio oaks. As I climbed the steps to the bell, the door flung open and Erasmus appeared.

I was ushered quickly into his library, a room containing a dizzying number of art works and artifacts that I assumed to be a well done collection of prints and replicas. After brief pleasantries and a glass of excellent wine, Mr. Milton briefly described his life history, and when he was done I thought the man insane. He calmly claimed to have entered King's College at the age of sixteen, in the same class as Alexander Hamilton. He then recited a litany of events where he claimed to be either a friend of, an enemy of, an aid for, or contemporary of nearly every major figure of the revolutionary period.

It didn't end there. His story included his participation in nearly every seminal event of American history since the end of the revolutionary war.

Trying to be polite, I told him I was impressed with his grasp of history and his storytelling, but that I really must go. "I don't expect you to believe me, my boy. You are a historian. But if you wish to see for yourself, if you have the courage, then come with me." He then led me up an old spiral staircase to his attic.

There, in that dusty old upper room, for the balance of the day and late into the night, the old man produced letters, papers, notes, and documents establishing his credentials. He indeed had a degree from King's, having there studied with and befriended a young patriot named Alexander Hamilton. He was indeed at Saratoga, wounded there, in fact. Later he corresponded with and acted as a clerk for Hamilton during the Constitutional Convention and later at the first Treasury Department. He assisted in the compiling of "The Federalist Papers", allowing his friend Alexander to bask in the glory of the ideas while he,

Erasmus, saw to the grammar, punctuation, and the legendary speed of completion.

He grieved for his best friend Hamilton when he was cut down by "that rascal Burr," as he invariably referred to Hamilton's nemesis.

Erasmus rarely commented on the strange fact that he was still here, saying only that he found it "rather odd" that someone would seem to "inherit a slower process of aging" which he said began about the time of Hamilton's death. He thought perhaps that it was due to his habit of bathing daily in cold water, a ritual once learned from Benjamin Franklin. He chuckled also that, until recently, it had been his practice to take advantage of any and all opportunities to "share the gift of granting pleasures" to any willing female accomplice. He was jovial in discussing his slow aging process. But in these jests I detected a defense mechanism shielding him from many a sadness. This old man no doubt had lost many friends, and I remember at the time that it was no surprise that he seemed so eager to impose himself with such speed and confidence into my home, my family, and my life.

I came to know that Erasmus would rarely delve into his own biography. In most cases he spoke of his own history only when prodded or motivated by emotion. But in this our first full day together his goal was to convince me of his odd reality. So he made an exception and in doing so he forever altered my life.

Apparently he lived and prospered in New York, witnessed the growth of the nation, moved his business interests to Albany and the Hudson River Valley, and eventually to Ohio. Having acquired all the wealth one could ever need, he settled in this tiny village and began once again to write.

I came to understand that Erasmus was still smarting from what he felt was the injustice of having been left out of the historical credits of the war, the early government, and most of all any credit for the writing of the famous "Federalist Papers".

While his friends Hamilton, Jay, and Madison had achieved immortality, the title of Founding Father had eluded him.

He felt he merited being held in such company, having participated in nearly all the prerequisite events. I believe it was this desire, above all, that drove him again to the pen.

Erasmus Milton was, however, no dinosaur. He was as educated, in touch, and insightful concerning the events of my time as he was of his own. In fact, while I wanted to talk for hours about his early life in the revolutionary cause, he would, for the most part, talk only of the issues of the day. In response to my continual pleading for interviews concerning his past, he elicited from me this promise. First I would assist him in the publications of his own "federalist essays" in the local paper, and then in book form, as were his beloved "Federalist Papers". Then, as part of this process, he would allow any and all interviews about his past, in any format I would choose. I, of course, quickly assented, not knowing the task to which I had committed myself.

But I can say with all sincerity that I loved old Erasmus Milton, and the publishing of his essays is the crown jewel of my academic life.

It should be noted that Erasmus, in keeping with the decorum of his time, wrote under a pseudonym. This eighteenth century practice was common, and the Founders often published under the name of some philosopher or historical figure. His good friend Alexander Hamilton, for example, wrote under the pseudonym "Plubius".

Erasmus chose to write under the name of an obscure first century Roman philosopher named Tacitus. I once challenged Erasmus on this issue, asserting that the Founders were practicing false modesty. "They simply wanted to show off their education and knowledge of such persons of antiquity" I chided. He protested, saying, "If a gentleman is offered a position of power, or the opportunity to influence others in print, he should go there humbly and incognito. He should go in fear of the impact his judgments and opinions may have on his reputation and his honor. When offered power or influence, it is good form to accept reluctantly."

It became Erasmus' practice to leave essays unexpectedly at my home, slipped through the front door mail slot by some student errand boy in the middle of the night. There were times when this system was quite comical, as the time where Erasmus had cajoled a young student athlete into a late night trip in violation of training rules. I had to have in this case a special meeting with the poor boy's coach, attended by Erasmus as well. My old friend concocted a fascinating and complicated tale of a late night historical mission, and then bought the boy's redemption with a case of old scotch and a football signed by Knute Rockne.

Hence the next morning I found his first essay lying in the front hallway. As promised, I then had the unenviable task of convincing the little local paper's editor to print the work, which I did by pretending Erasmus was a significant historical re-enactor and writer from New England. When it was published as an editorial that week in the Lafayette Weekly News Gazette for July of 2004, it was signed only "Tacitus." This obscure pseudonym seems odd, but he told me that some day I would read the works of his literary namesake and I would come across a quote that would explain his choice.

Why he began where he did in his essays was a mystery. I know now that he was none too happy with the tone of debate in American politics, as it reminded him much of the tenor of the factional political wars between Hamilton and Jefferson. He felt anger and hatred were to political discourse as oil and water, I sense a belief he came to out of personal experience and time. In any case, he eloquently stated this position in his first essay, which he titled, "The Presidency." Never again did I meet with any resistance from the editor of the Lafayette Weekly News Gazette.

The Presidency

I have lived a long time, and seen many things. It has been the fortunate circumstance of my life to have known men who became presidents. I can say as well that I have been friends with some other men who should have been. How this is true, or if you believe it to be true, is not germane to the issue. I do not write of these gentlemen, but of the office they were honored with. This invention of our constitution is an office that each was temporarily entrusted with, and we are blessed by Providence with the opportunity to periodically help select it's next caretaker.

It is first important to note that every man inhabiting that office has been, to some degree, an imperfect personage. Some lacked personal discipline, others competence, others honor in their affairs. But they all inhabited "the office." We Americans are somewhat like the Popish church. Among their various odd traditions is the tradition that all popes can be traced back to Peter. We know as a matter of history, however, that all presidents can be traced back to Washington. There is a thread that runs through the souls of all who inhabit this office, and that thread attaches them back into time, through Lincoln, through Monroe, through Jefferson, and ultimately to Washington.

I say this because it has become, in the tenor of our time, acceptable for those who would call themselves patriots to treat with contempt those who have, by the providence of history, taken their turn in this office.

I would say clearly to such "patriots" that they are wrong in doing so. I see this phenomenon with our current chief of state. His opponents do not disagree with our current president; they despise him. Were he to propose a bill that designated the sky to be blue, those damned Jeffersonians would filibuster it and swear him to be wrong.

And his predecessor was not treated any better. Mr. Clinton conducted his personal affairs in a way that, while not admirable, would not have merited a second mention in the parlors and chambers of my youth. Yet his opponents, self-righteous as Lincolnites tend to be, sought to overthrow the government over an affair more appropriately rebuked by a scorned wife than a court of impeachment.

Much as I had my disagreements with Jefferson and his anti-federalists, their leader was right and true in his beliefs about democracy. It is good and healthy that we disagree, that we debate, and that, in the end, we agree to act. When we vote in a leader then he becomes ours. While we debate him still, we also respect the office he holds and him as long as he holds it. I am suggesting that it is time Americans grow up. Do you believe in democracy or not? If not, let us once again anoint ourselves a king. If you do, then start also believing in your opponent's right to disagree with you, and the chance that, just occasionally, he may be right.

Tacitus

Chapter Two
Remember Eliza, You
are a Christian

By August of 2004, I had convinced our local paper editor, a young Ohio Northern graduate named Jared Walsh for whom I occasionally wrote, to publish the essays of my old friend as a series. This young grandchild of Irish immigrants had at first wanted nothing to do with the idea, but as noted earlier was won over by the first essay. The idea of a series was an easier sale, especially when combined with regular meetings with the author and gifts of finely aged Irish whiskey.

Upon learning of this small victory, Erasmus began to replicate the incredible pace of his claimed close associate Hamilton, who had produced the "Federalist" essays at a pace of some twenty five per month. Erasmus wrote of things he found odd or particularly inaccurate about the intent of the Founders. Hence his second essay attacked the current distortions about Jefferson and his infamous "wall of separation."

It has become common knowledge, of course, that Jefferson first used this term in a private letter. Erasmus, being in the clique of federalists surrounding Hamilton and Washington, distained it at the timed, and distained it still. He nearly came to blows with Jefferson in a confrontation at the newly formed Department of State, telling Jefferson "you have no idea the damage you have done".

"Remember Eliza, you are a Christian."

⤬

Sometimes it is painful to live so long as to lose touch with the intellectual elite, especially when one once counted himself a member. But true pain lies in recollections of friends long dead, memories long faded, and fond remembrances that stubbornly resist the kind forgetfulness of age.

One such moment is my remembrance of the day my good and dear friend Hamilton kept his ill-fated appointment with that scoundrel and traitor, Burr. I drove the coach bearing my friend to that awful field, and I jolted at hearing the first shot which Hamilton aimed intentionally high. He did so to spare Burr's life and preserve his own honor. Burr, unencumbered by such notions as honor, sent his ball into the brilliant patriot's noble heart. As we raced back to his home, with my Hamilton mortally wounded, his life oozed away. I carried him in my arms to his bed, and wept with his wife as he lay dying in his room. With some difficulty and not a little persuasion, he had imposed on the local Anglican to give him the final sacraments. My beloved Hamilton was always to some degree a religious man.

But as it is with all men of intellect, it took time for him to understand that it is not for us, nor should it be, to understand all things. As his mind made peace with this fact, his soul moved closer to where his wife Eliza had always been, and closer to God. His final words to his wife, seeing her grief and fear, were "Remember Eliza, you are a Christian."

Like my friend Hamilton, my beloved republic has had a strange and changeable relationship with God. But I find it misleading bordering on the dishonorable, that for purposes of more modern political agendas and an apparent desire to eliminate all modesty, discretion, and restriction on personal behavior, many have taken to denying the profound relationship the Founders had with their God.

11

Jefferson's one mention of that silly "wall" between church and state has been abused into a weapon to try to make our judiciary anti-Christian. My personal knowledge of the men of the times has me know that even Jefferson's main concern was that no one would be forced to worship, and that no government would favor one denomination over another. Were he to know now that judges have empowered the central government to tell the elected officials of every hamlet and village what they can and cannot do in their own villages, towns, schools, and courtrooms, on religion or any other matter, I dare say that this anti-federalist Founder would say it is time once again to "water the roots of the tree of liberty with the blood of patriots."

Granted, Thomas was always willing to shed blood as long as it wasn't his own, but he feared the central authority more than the local mob. Were he to know that his words were being used by the central power to quash the rule of the local, his pen would burn hot indeed.

Another Virginian, our dearest and most honorable General Washington, more rightly stated for posterity the correct role of government in religious life. In his final and farewell address before he reassumed the role of our own Cincinnatus, he gave us three warnings: first, to avoid foreign alliances; second, to not form political parties. Because of our government's unfortunate hostility to religion, these are the only two taught to our children in school. But the dear General saved the most important warning for last; here is what he said:

"Of all the dispositions and habits which lead to political prosperity, religion and morality are indispensable supports. In vain would that man claim the tribute of patriotism who would labor to subvert these great pillars of human happiness, these firmest props of the duties of men and citizens. The mere politician, equally with the pious man, ought to respect and to cherish them. A volume could not trace all their connections with private and public felicity. Let it simply be asked, where is the security for property, for reputation, for life, if the sense of religious obligation desert the oaths which are the instruments of investigation in the courts of justice?

And let us with caution indulge the supposition that morality can be maintained without religion. Whatever can be conceded to the influence of refined education on the minds of peculiar structure, reason and experience both forbid us to expect that national morality can prevail in exclusion of religious principle."

Who can doubt that the "decline in national morality" and our judiciary's war against religion have not corresponded? Is it not possible to heed Jefferson's warning to avoid forced piety, and still encourage that which we know to be good and beneficial for our society? Perhaps our beloved Washington did for the Union as he passed away from public life what Hamilton did for his dear Eliza. Perhaps he was saying to his own beloved country, "Remember, Eliza, you are a Christian."

Tacitus

Chapter Three
The New Royalty

It became evident to me over time that Erasmus was a man of means, although at the time I had no idea of the extent of his wealth. He had an active business and legal career that spanned the two centuries of his adulthood, so it came as no surprise that he was by no means a poor man. For several days that August, I questioned him about his business experience, and in early September, as we sat on the veranda of his stately home, his mind wandered back to the beginning. It seems that after Hamilton's death, Erasmus Milton left the practice of law and became successful running river packets and trade up the Hudson to Albany. As capital, he used a significant fortune he had made buying federal debt at huge discounts before Hamilton became Treasury Secretary. There was significant controversy surrounding this first fortune, and Erasmus was more than a little sheepish in recounting how he had suffered blistering attacks from anti-federalists both in the press and personally because of his trading in state revolutionary war debt soon to be assumed by the new government. I began to see the pattern of the old man's temper as he told of a confrontation with James Madison on the senate floor. "That hypocrite abandoned both Hamilton and our dear old General, recanted on his federalist writings before ratification, and then accused me of dishonorable conduct in my financial affairs. Were it not for my lecturing of Alexander about the absurdity of duels, I would have fought one my self that day" Erasmus thundered.

As a connected individual and early investor in "Clinton's Ditch," Erasmus again benefited from being involved in the planning and expanding of the new nation. He already had transports, goods, and places of exchange in place on Lake Erie even before the Hudson and Erie Canal was completed. So a second fortune was secured.

By the days of the "Robber Barons" of the Gilded Age, Erasmus Milton hobnobbed with the Astors, Carnegies, and Morgans, then the Fisks, Rockefellers, Vanderbilts, and Fords. In the summer, his canal boats and trains would run rich Hudson River families to Erie, where his Erie steamers would deliver them to the Hotel Breakers on Sandusky Bay. There he would dine with America's new royalty, plot how to make more profit, and listen to Edison crow about his latest idea.

In the fall, that same group would take Henry Flagler's train to St. Augustine, and exchange the Erie breezes of summer for the warm Atlantic breezes of winter. Erasmus was ambivalent about these times. He never expressed regret about his success, and said often he was no "carriage communist." He took special pride in creating employment, and there were few things he honored more than work. Yet I often felt his wealth was like an ill-fitted suit that he wore at times with some discomfort. Therefore, the tone of his next essay was not a complete surprise.

"Robber Barons"

If there is a time of my life I regret, it must be the years dawdling away in lazy wealth, during what uninformed historians have dubbed the Gilded Age. This was the period before the income tax, yet after industrialization, where more wealth was amassed in a matter of years than had ever existed in all the economies of the world to date. I was no fan of the anti-federalist crowd. I held in contempt their desire for a simple, weak, agrarian country of slave-owning farmer gentlemen. Nevertheless, I must give Jefferson credit on this point: It is indeed easy to forget one's duty when one has too much wealth and ease.

Having lived through the time prior to our constitution, and having seen with my own eyes the near loss of all our gains of the revolution during the Confederation period, I am less quick to assign only ill designs to the power of the central government.

During the debates over the currency, the assumption of debt, and the creation of the central bank, at which time I was writing speeches and whipping up votes for my dear friend Mr. Hamilton, we often discussed the appropriate use of the central power. Unlike the anti-federalists, we modern students of governance thought there was a role to play for a sound but non-intrusive central authority in building the wealth of nations.

One evening at The Breakers, I listened to John Rockefeller flailing away at this young new President Roosevelt. As he droned on, my conversations with my beloved Hamilton about the appropriateness of central government power drifted in and out of my mind. You see, John was more than a little displeased at the amount of legal fees it was costing him to keep his oil monopoly from being rent asunder, and this "Reform

Republican" was to blame. Not particularly liking John anyway, bombastic and arrogant bastard that he was, I decided to take my next ship to Buffalo and cruise down to Albany to meet this self-proclaimed "Trust Buster". On the way, I boned up on my Adam Smith, especially those areas where capitalist efficiencies flourished only where markets remained free.

My dinner with Theodore, with whom I became fast friends, was enchanting. Such ideas! A central authority that would secure the integrity of exchanges and insure adequate competition for goods and services. Legal authority to bust up monopolies. Workman's compensation, safe factories, restrictions on child labor, national parks, conservation. No wonder John loathed this man so.

Now, note he was no fan of government control. Teddy was as far from a socialist as one could come. He believed, as I still do, that taxes, regulation, and government power are necessary evils to be minimized. And a government can do no more an unwise or harmful thing than to try to force a leveling of society by turning against its men of industry, business, and property.

However, the concept that government can at times help people and should be allowed to do so—the idea intrigued me.

Now granted there has probably been more harm done by government in its ill-fated attempts to help people than in any other way. But this man Theodore, he opened my mind a bit that evening in Albany. And a mind in such a state of openness is necessary when one's body has, for whatever odd reason, decided to ignore time.

Tacitus

Chapter Four
The Feud

As the end of summer approached, I became more attached to my old friend. It is hard to explain, but intellectually I simply did not deal with the fact that this man, by all evidence, was nearly a two and a half centuries old. Neither did he, save an occasional comment or joke about this most unbelievable fact. I hid the fact of his age from my friend Mr. Walsh at the paper, not wanting the novelty of his age to overshadow the wonderfulness of his words. Nor did I need to be continually having to prove the fact, knowing that process would never end. It was easy to convince Mr. Walsh that Erasmus was simply using a literary technique to add historical flavor to his works. Besides, the young editor knew a story when he saw one, and he believed whatever I told him so long as he got to meet periodically with Erasmus at his home and sample the contents of his bar and humidor.

Erasmus had a timeless wit and always wanted to talk about current events. I, on the other hand, had the incredible good fortune to befriend a man who was a contemporary of the Founding Fathers, and unfortunately for the old man, I pestered him relentlessly for stories about Franklin, Hamilton, Washington, and the like. He didn't often indulge me, but occasionally I would strike a chord, and off he would go. It seemed his second favorite among the founding elite after his friend Hamilton was old Dr. Franklin.

In our time we would have called them "drinking buddies", and I believe Erasmus' habit of flirting relentlessly in his old age was acquired from Franklin.

There was one evening in particular where I mentioned a reverence for Jefferson and a lack of understanding as to why Erasmus' friend Hamilton had despised him so. We had an extended and animated discussion, and I found it fascinating to realize that this group of men was not monolithic. They had their clicks, their likes, and their dislikes. In Erasmus' case, I got a distinct feeling that he felt compelled to side with Hamilton as a matter of loyalty, and his respect for Jefferson barely overcame his dislike for him. This is not to say that Erasmus actively tried to undermine Jefferson like Hamilton had done. Nor did he attack him in public press. The virulent nature of the political press at that time greatly offended my friend, and he often chided his friend Alexander for participating. It was Jefferson's clandestine attacks in that press on the old General that drove a permanent dislike of him into Erasmus' mind. Everyone knew at the time that Washington was to be spared these political attacks. He was "off limits", and Jefferson violated this rule. It was this act, not his simplistic anti federalist agrarianism, that Erasmus could never forgive. As was often the case after a long evening discussion, later that night Erasmus sent yet another student on a mission of great importance, and another envelope slid through the mail slot onto my hallway floor.

Jefferson

It has been said, mostly by those who were not privy to the private thoughts of either man, that my good friend Hamilton and the Virginian Jefferson so detested one another as to have their mutual interchange best described as hatred. I have had many years to think and rethink the nature, abilities, and exchanges of these two titans, and I think this characterization is unfair.

It must be understood, first of all, that my dear Alexander did not view Jefferson at the beginning as a pivotal member of that inner circle of giants who established America. While Hamilton served on Washington's staff and stormed Yorktown redoubts with Lafayette at his side, Jefferson saw no action during the war. This is not to say that it is right to hold his revolutionary period in contempt, but he did not, like Hamilton, exit the revolution as a war hero. It is fair, in fact, to say that Hamilton during this period hardly knew him.

While Hamilton teamed with Jay and Madison (and I dare say with invaluable, yet unfortunately unrecognized, contributions from your humble servant) to pressure New York into the ratification camp, Jefferson was in France. Instead of aiding in the ratification of the new governing document, he wondered aloud from his distant Paris apartments if the Constitution was complete without a "Bill of Rights".

And while Hamilton was serving again with our old general, and inventing our government as the first Secretary of the Treasury, Jefferson was a late arrival at State. So it can be said that initially Hamilton had little contact with, and no particular opinion about, Jefferson.

There were things in common about these two men. First of all, they were brilliant. Secondly, they were patriots.

Jefferson gave birth to the "idea" of America. "We hold these truths to be self-evident." Imagine, if you will, first espousing the concept that a people will say together to their king that there is truth that rises above power, rights that rise above kings and princes, and justice that is so right as to rise above even argument and challenge. Truth that is so right in its own nature that it is self-evident. This concept to you, having heard it for two centuries in your schools and on your July day of celebration, is old and obvious. But not then, when this Virginia planter first gave it life and breath.

And what of "inalienable rights"? Jefferson took these enlightenment concepts of Locke and Smith, of private property and self-rule, and carried them to the throne of God himself. He obtained there a blessing, and returned to us with "life, liberty, and the pursuit of happiness." This was Jefferson's gift.

And what of my friend Alexander? His light shone brightest in making the "Idea" of America a reality.

His campaign to save ratification gave us the constitution upon which a Bill of Rights could be grafted. And he was the engineer who built the government that endures today. His public credit, his national bank, his payment of revolutionary debt, his treasury department, his custom taxes and trade treaties, his promotion of infrastructure and manufactures. Upon his arrival at the Constitutional Convention, there was nothing. By the end of his service, there was a complete and functional government. He gave Jefferson's words structure and form, functionality and permanence. That was Hamilton's gift.

So what of this feud? It is safe to say that neither man at the time would agree with my backward looking understanding. But Jefferson, I now understand, had no fear of the mob. He would welcome disorder as long as liberty was found safe. He feared only kings, central power, and the shadow of tyrants. Such was the depth of his fear that he would abandon a Lafayette and embrace a Robespierre.

As Hamilton built a central government, Jefferson could not see the need for liberty to reign with order. He could see only a threat in any government power, and to this threat he attached a face. That face was of our beloved Hamilton.

And Alexander's flaw was similar. His fear was of disunion, of the country being torn apart by those who would keep us in a perpetual state of revolution, where a country was not possible because all men were forever in rebellion. Hamilton feared disorder. He feared mob rule. He feared Jefferson.

Jefferson came, in his life, to acknowledge Hamilton, if not to revere him. The power provided by Hamilton was used by Jefferson to expand our borders, fight pirates, and explore frontiers. Hate? Perhaps at the time we thought it was so. But not now. Scream "Revisionist!" at me if you must, but you were not there. These two men loved what America could become, and they both had a hand in its becoming. So I have forgiven them their feud in this life, and they each other in the next. We would not be here were it not for them both, and for that they deserve our discretion in leaving the historical stone of their mutual animosities unturned. Hence I will not speak again of their lack of love for each other, but only of their mutual love for their country.

Tacitus

Chapter Five
The Colby Boys

There are many things about my relationship with Erasmus Milton which must seem odd to you, the reader of his published essays. No doubt first among these items is his age, which if his stories are to be believed, puts his date of birth somewhere in the late 1750s. I came to accept this fact, I suppose, because after a while acceptance came as natural to me as it did to him.

Odd as this issue may seem, there was to me a coincidence even less likely than having met a 248-year-old lost "Founding Father" in Lafayette, Ohio. It seems that a small, respected, and beautiful little college in central Maine had played an unlikely role in both our lives. For me, it is where my endlessly adventurous older son Timothy had decided to attend college, study history and economics, and play football for the Colby College White Mules. I visited him there many times, and fell hopelessly in love with this jewel of American history and education.

As seemed always the case, Erasmus' experience at Colby was deeper and infinitely more interesting. One evening, when I mentioned my son's college to him, he said he knew it well. It seems there is a bell in the bell tower there that was cast and provided by the son of Paul Revere, from the Revere family metal works in Boston. "Did you know this son?" I asked.

"Only in passing," he said, "but I knew his father quite well."

Erasmus then told the story of his own relationship with Colby College. Around the turn of the nineteenth century he acquired interest in the lumber industry. He talked of watching from Mayflower Hill as the log floats from his cut timber stands rumbled down the Kennebec River, through the small town of Waterville, to his shipyards in Portland and Bath. There he built his armada of coastal sloops and river barges that would earn him his second fortune. It is in this town, in 1813, that he attended a meeting to assist a group of Boston and Portland gentlemen in the founding of what was to become Colby College.

There was more to Colby and Erasmus, and I could feel it in him as he spoke, but it was not until another evening that I found out what this extra dimension was. I was reading an article about the "slavery reparations" debate, and was struck by a civil rights leader's comment that the North fought to save the Union, not to free the slaves. Knowing Erasmus Milton to have been, at the time, a radical abolitionist, I read him the article and asked him what he thought of the concept and the statement.

"It may have been so with some," he said. "You know, I went to your son's college, Colby, in 1863. I went to hear a great poet and abolitionist leader, a man named Ralph Waldo Emerson.

He gave the commencement address there that spring. If this man you told me of, if he could have heard Emerson that day, I think it would change his mind."

I sensed that my friend was hurt by the civil rights leader's remark about the Union's motivation for the Civil War. He was not a person to take slights without retort or contain his temper, but in this case he quietly took the charge in an oddly personal way. It was like he knew people who had indeed felt otherwise, and it was no surprise that another essay soon appeared on my hallway floor, beneath the old mail slot.

The Colby Boys

❦

As I contemplate the ugliest chapter in the history of America, my mind travels backwards to another time. For a man of my age, this happens often, and it is both pleasant and sometimes painful. I am contemplating slavery, our fight against it, and its ultimate cost. As I do so, I come again to where I was years ago, in what must be the most beautiful place in the world.

I am in New England, central Maine to be exact, at Colby College. Princeton, an intellectual rival to the south, publishes a review each year, identifying Colby as one of the most beautiful campuses in America. This campus sits on the crest of Mayflower Hill, high above the town of Waterville, an old mill village which sits astride the historic Kennebec River.

Readers from my adopted hamlet of Lafayette, being from the Midwest, would be struck by what must seem to them as the ancient history of this place. The Kennebec river valley was the route used by Arnold to lead a patriot army to Canada.

The college itself was founded less than forty years after Jefferson's pen gave birth to our Declaration of Independence. Its first students studied there just nine years after my dear Hamilton fell victim to his unfortunate preoccupation with lesser men's insults. The bell in the Colby bell tower is still in use there, being skillfully crafted by the son of Paul Revere. For over 200 years, logs cut from the Maine forests were floated down the Kennebec River, past the Colby campus, and onto the shipyards of Bath and Portland. These famous shipyards turned out sturdy Yankee vessels that plied the Atlantic trade, a trade dominated by Caribbean sugar, European manufactures, and African slaves.

New England bore a collective feeling of guilt for our indirect participation in the slave trade, a participation about which southern leaders from Patrick Henry to John Calhoun were always ready to remind us. This guilt and desire for redemption, in no small degree, led our region to become hotly abolitionist, and Maine was no exception.

Having retreated to Maine after Hamilton's death to seek the solace of the mind that such a place can provide, it was here, at Colby, that I found voice to my hatred of the slave trade and the infernal contradictions it presented to men who saw liberty as the goal of our sacred revolution. In 1826 I met there a student named Elijah Lovejoy, an abolitionist student radical. He was later murdered by a pro-slavery mob in Alton, Illinois, on November 7, 1837.

His crime was refusing to cease the publication of his abolitionist newspaper, and he died, martyred for abolition, at the foot of his press.

He had proclaimed in his paper, "I have sworn eternal opposition to slavery, and by the blessing of God, I shall never go back." A plaque displaying these words hangs in his honor on the wall of the Lorimer Chapel, a stunning New England church structure that lovingly hovers over her students walking daily across the Colby campus.

Down the slope from the Lorimer Chapel, in front of the equally stunning library, is an old granite monument inscribed with the names of Colby graduates who died in the great and terrible Civil War. There were seventeen students and ten alumni listed there, names of boys whose families I knew and loved. This number of souls, sacrificed on the alter of freedom, represented nearly ten percent of the population of the tiny campus.

By 1860 Maine had grown ever more radically abolitionist, and she contributed mightily in both men and resources to the Union cause. Many people came from many places to serve in the Union army, and they came for many reasons. But let there be no mistake: the sons of Maine, and the boys from Colby, they went to free the slaves.

By now my business interests had drawn me back to Albany. Then, with the coming of the war, I again offered my sword to liberty's cause, and found myself again in a staff position attached to Lincoln's war department.

It was an agreeable duty that reminded me of my previous service with Hamilton on the staff of our old beloved General Washington. During this period, I read some of the works of a hero of abolition and famous author, poet, and philosopher, Ralph Waldo Emerson.

When I heard he was to speak at Colby College, the site of both my healing and my enlightenment, I begged leave and headed north. On August 11 of 1863, he spoke words that still are inscribed at the base of the flagpole at the center of the Colby campus. These words made New England's sentiments clear: "Who would not, if it could be more certain that a new morning of universal liberty should rise on our race by the perishing of one generation, who among us would not consent to die?"

Again I state clearly that the twenty-seven Colby boys went off not to fight against states' rights, or to avenge Fort Sumter, or to save the Union. They went as abolitionists, as did I, to end slavery, to honor the sacrifice of Elijah Lovejoy, and to pursue Emerson's "morning of universal liberty."

Who could of known, as we went off to war in 1861, how close we would come to Emerson's chilling assessment of the cost of liberty, how close indeed to the death of an entire generation. Yet it could be said that having declared in 1776 that "all men are created equal," this ocean of death was a just penance for a land that tolerated the evil of slavery for so long.

This penance was harsh indeed, and it littered the road to our national redemption with the bodies of these Colby boys, and the 20th Maine, and hundreds of thousands of other boys from every northern state.

It is said now by some that more is needed, that the ancestors of slaves should be paid reparations. But where along this bloody road, this hollowed ground, shall we find a place for civil suits and cash payments? To do so we must accept the concept of liability that travels across time from generation to generation. This concept is not of the new world, but of the old. It is the kind of thinking that does not allow the children of a people wronged to forgive and embrace the children of the wrong doers and then move on.

The idea of reparations is the kind of thinking that allows Irish Catholics and Protestants, Serbs and Croats, Boers and Zulus, Arabs and Jews to teach their children of ancient feuds and hate and senseless killing. Such thinking engenders conflict that never ends. It is not, and should not be our way.

If we owe a debt to the ancestors of slaves, it is most appropriately paid by bringing to pass that of which the founders wrote, that all men are indeed created equal. Our down payment on reparations was made at Shiloh, Cold Harbor, Gettysburg, and Antietam. More installments were made through constitutional amendments, voting rights acts, freedom rides, and affirmative action.

Every time an American embraces a person of another color, accepts a family intermarried, provides an opportunity for success to a minority youth, or shows offense at a racial jest, he honors abolition and makes another payment. And we should go on making payments such as these until equality arrives.

But private reparations for specific deeds still unforgiven? No, that cannot be the way. Reparations is the path of anger, of hate, of non-forgiveness, and of generational animosity.

And if we choose this path, who then should be paid? Surely the ancestors of southern slaves, but what then of the one million free black soldiers who served the Union in the United States Colored Troops? What of the ancestors of Elijah Lovejoy and other martyrs to the cause of abolition? And what of the descendents of the twenty-seven Colby boys?

To say the debt created by slavery has been rendered paid is an awful abdication of the need to heal our collective national soul. Slavery is our unique national sin, and we must never forget the obligation it created. But this is not Ireland, or the Balkans, or Palestine, or Africa. We are all Americans, all of us from somewhere else, and whether on the Mayflower itself or in the belly of a wretched slave ship, we are better off for our ancestors having come here.

So let us remember, but let us forgive. Let us seek justice, not compensation. Let us seek healing, not vengeance. Let us tarnish neither the suffering of former slaves nor the sacrifice of those who died to free them. Their memory will find no glory in the civil courts of greed and injustice where men in the profession of Hamilton, Jefferson, and Lincoln now ply their trade like hawkers of snake oil, encouraging neighbors to sue one another.

Instead, let us recommit together to that which we should have first accomplished: equal justice, equal rights, and equal opportunity. In this way, all reparations shall be paid, all forgiveness granted, and Emerson's "morning of universal liberty" will finally dawn.

Tacitus

Chapter Six
The Father of Rights

In the hopes of holding my dear Erasmus to his promise of unlimited interviews about his past, I often pestered him about the historic giants of our history, most of whom he seemed to have known. I provided him with new works on the lives of Hamilton, Jefferson, Washington, Lafayette, and Adams. He would consume the books with an amazing voracity, then critique them (or is correct a better word?). I would listen to his wonderful anecdotes about each Founder, and review reams of original notes and documents. I dare say I would learn more history walking with Erasmus for an afternoon across the campus of little Ohio Northern University than I did in three years of graduate school.

He steadfastly refused to state who he thought was the most important Founder, though I suspect he would have favored General Washington and his "beloved Hamilton."

I did entice him to discussion once by saying that many in our country felt that the right to food, or medical care, or an education were the most important rights. He scoffed at this notion, and retorted that to suggest that anyone was "entitled" to the product of anything produced by the sweat of another man's brow was "Jacobin nonsense."

Erasmus often used this term "Jacobin" as a reference for modern liberalism. He saw many commonalities between the French Revolution's contempt for order and property with modern liberalism's apparent belief that you are entitled to take from your neighbor via government taxation anything you need, whether you have earned it or not. He held any attempt to define rights and liberty in ways that relieved each person from the responsibility for his own well being in great distain.

"As my dear Hamilton said, my dear boy," Erasmus continued, "when a society turns against its men of property, liberty is doomed."

I teased him that modern liberals would call him heartless. "Heartless?" he exclaimed. "What could be more heartless than to convert our government to a giant wet nurse and then addict the people to her milk laden breasts? After she has us all suckling on the common teat, having destroyed not just our ability to earn our own way with work and merit, but even our desire to do so, can she not then order us about like a dominating, all powerful bitch? Always remember, the government would like nothing more than having all of us dependent on one program or another. Let me tell you this, my good man, no man is free who is dependent on the government for his daily bread. Not the pensioner, nor the indigent, nor the working man. If you do not make your own way, then you are a slave to those upon whose succor you depend."

This exchange was one of our most memorable. It clearly showed that this old abolitionist, while willing to help anyone, especially those of color, to succeed, he would truck no nonsense that allowed any individual a "free ride." It was no surprise that an equally entertaining and effervescent essay appeared the next morning in my post box.

The Father of Rights

There are, in this modern time, many things that are indeed greatly improved from those of times past. The current quality of life, of food, of medicine, and of communications is surely a great wonder to behold. I can say, however, that in one area we as a people seemed to have wandered from a better to a "less better" understanding.

When our odd yet brilliant founding philosopher from Virginia penned the documents that defined the soul of our "Glorious Cause", he correctly identified that there are three rights that are natural to man, and unalterable by government. Free peoples have the right to life, liberty, and property.

By "life," we have come to understand that a person cannot have his life, or his ability to live as he wishes in ways not harmful to others, taken away.

By "liberty," we mean he is entitled to speak his mind, publish his opinions, select his leaders, and assemble with his neighbors without unwarranted intrusions by others, including and especially his government.

By "property," we know that what a man produces, owns, builds, acquires via his own wit or wisdom, inheritance, investment or labor, is his own. He is free to improve the lot of himself and his family, and is not a serf owing his daily bread to a lord, whether that lord be a noble or a government. In other words, a free person has the right to be self-sufficient, self-dependent, even wealthy, if his circumstances or abilities so enable him.

It is this last right that I hold most dear, and most necessary. For no man is free who must depend on the government for his daily bread. And no person is entitled to any property, compensation, or service that he has not earned or cannot afford to purchase.

The public pensioner must vote for those who would protect his public pension, even if those leaders be tyrants. He has no choice. And the poor man, heartlessly destroyed and addicted to the public dole by his government, must vote for the person who will continue to dole out his free food and lodging, even if that person is a despot. He has no choice.

This does not mean that our nation should not be a nation of benevolence and charity. We are a rich country, and we should share our wealth with those in need. But such charity, when coerced on the giver, and when no requirement of effort at improvement and labor is imposed on the recipient, embitters the former and destroys the latter. Such is the nature of benevolence imposed upon us by the power of government. It embitters those who would otherwise help, and destroys those to whom help is given.

Free men will chose benevolence, as they will also choose good leaders, if their private property rights are protected. This is proven over and over again by the amazing level of private benevolence given by our citizens since the founding of the nation. Yet it seems the goal of Jacobins and their historical heirs (socialists, communists, liberals, and the like) to destroy the self-sufficiency of the people and addict them all to the distributions of bread from the central authority. If this is ever accomplished, and our society first vilifies, then rejects, then turns on its men of property, then liberty will be no more.

Tacitus

Chapter Seven
The Treaty of Elena

On a beautiful Sunday afternoon in the fall of 2004, I walked with my wife Beda and Erasmus through the little village of Lafayette. We were accompanied by my seventeen-year-old daughter Stephanie, and my ten-year-old son Matthew. We followed what had become, since summer, our normal course, down the lane from his home to the main street, past the old veteran's monument and its lovely old statues of civil war soldiers, and back to his home again.

During our walks Erasmus often indulged in the prerogative of an older man, engaging in flirtation and charming exchanges with Beda. This had been true since their first meeting. Erasmus had a special affection for my family, and a particular fondness for little Matthew. They read often together, and had recently taken to fishing in the small pond on Erasmus' property. There was a special bond developing between the old man and the boy.

Today in his conversations with Beda he dwelt as he often did on her immigrant status, her experiences coming to America from Mexico, and all things "Spanish" about her and her heritage. They would most often converse in Spanish, in which Erasmus was fluent. After a long exchange between them, and as Erasmus moved ahead to join Matthew in the relentless pursuit of a butterfly, I questioned Beda with the inevitable "What did he say?"

"He was commenting on how pretty Stephanie is, and how much she looks like me," Beda teased. "He said God had made an error not placing Eden on the Rio, as there were already two angels there."

"What a flirt," I said.

"What a dear old gentleman," she replied.

We watched Matthew and Erasmus walking ahead of us. When Matt wasn't chasing some stray cat or pursuing some flying insect, he would place his hand on old Erasmus' shoulder and walk at his side. He had of late taken to calling Erasmus "Papa Milton," a development that seemed to please them both. After the now frequent dinners at my house, the two of them would doze together on my couch in the library. This room contained all my books, our family piano, and walls covered with various and sundry historical scenes and art prints of famous Americans. At some time in the family history it had been dubbed the "Smart Room" by the children, as being in the room made you "smart".

Often after dinner, Erasmus would announce to Matthew, "It would now be appropriate for all gentlemen to retire to your father's "smart room" to exercise our minds and contemplate the issues of our time." Matthew would then laugh and grab Erasmus' hand, dragging him to the library for an evening of books, stories, and tall tales about the men whose pictures line the "smart room" walls.

Erasmus' tenderness toward my wife and family made me curious about his own family, as did the myriad of small portraits and tint types that I regularly came across while perusing the relics of his attic. This curiosity, of course, bettered me, and I asked him once why he had never married.

"You have applied to me the constraints of a normal life span, my boy, and in doing so have again jumped to an incorrect conclusion," he replied. I took this to mean he had married, and I realized that there was an entire other part of my friend's life about which I knew nothing. He did not seem to mind my inquisition, so I asked about his family. The story he then told to me was as beautiful, touching, and melancholy a tale as I have ever heard. It made clear why my dear old friend was always so smitten by my wife and family, and deepened my empathy for his plight. Allow me to share it with you now.

As you may recall, Erasmus Milton had claimed to serve as the Under Secretary to Alexander Hamilton, in the very first Treasury Department. The Senate, jealous of Mr. Hamilton's influence with President Washington, had tried to slow his pace by requiring mountains of reports and statistics on all of his initiatives. Hence Erasmus was forced to reprise his role as the ghost editor of the Federalist Papers, editing and perfecting a myriad of Hamilton's replies to congressional inquiries on the assumption of state war debt, the national bank, the tariffs and duties taxation, and the acquisition of foreign and domestic credit.

Alexander and Erasmus had shepherded all these proposals through a reluctant congress, and as a result had achieved the goal of sound credit for the new central government.

Jefferson's cabal were increasingly hostile to Washington's government, and conspired with Federalists, increasingly afraid of Hamilton's growing power, to slow him down by keeping him busy with their ever growing demands for reports. It was during this period that Hamilton and Jefferson became rivals. Later, when Jefferson assisted in public attacks on the old General, it is fair to say that they became enemies.

It is also fair to say that Hamilton was the most powerful man in the new government, and at times felt himself if not the only capable member, at least the most capable one. Given his role in negotiating foreign loans, he felt empowered to constantly further antagonize Jefferson by encroaching on his turf as Secretary of State.

Jefferson, who was no doubt a patriot, was also paranoid that any central government powerful enough to govern would lead to tyranny. He felt that a people constantly in a state of agitated revolution, with all the associated disorder and bloodletting, was the best way to ward off tyrants. He was then a constant apologist for the Jacobin French revolution, despite its horrors and abuses.

Hamilton was equally a patriot, and felt his revolutionary credentials superior to Jefferson's since he had lent his sword and repeatedly nearly lost his life in service to the "Glorious Cause". He also abhorred mob rule, and felt the rule of law and the preservation of the Constitution were liberty's only hope.

It should be no surprise then that these two men were in a constant state of agitation and competitive intrigue. So when Hamilton asked Erasmus Milton to accompany him to the Spanish diplomatic mission in the growing embassy area of Philadelphia, Erasmus could be forgiven for fearing that another fight would soon be brewing between his good friend Hamilton and Secretary Jefferson.

Erasmus was full of such misgivings as he and Hamilton took a late night coach ride to the home of a Spanish diplomat, which served as an unofficial embassy of the Spanish crown. As Hamilton knocked on the door, Erasmus again pleaded with him to at least keep Jefferson apprised of his activities. This thought was the last one Erasmus was to have that evening that had anything to do with his official duties. For as the door opened, there standing before him, serving as the lady of the house, was the seventeen-year-old daughter of Enriquez Garza, secret personal emissary to America from the Kingdom of Spain.

Her name was Elena, and she was, in Erasmus' words, "as stunning as your own beautiful wife and daughter, with the lovely brown eyes, tan skin, and brown hair of her people."

There is little doubt that Hamilton was equally smitten, but as he was already married to his dear Eliza and was there on a mission that would enhance his own growing stature, he uncharacteristically deferred to his friend.

Hamilton and Garza disappeared into the private study, while Erasmus stayed behind. Neither he nor Elena took any note of the evening's intense negotiations. Hamilton did indeed obtain additional credit for the young government, but not in the amounts or at the terms hoped for. He did not mind the minor set back, as the loan request had been a secondary goal. His intrigue of the evening, and the real reason for the late night adventure, was to attempt to negotiate a treaty that would add Florida as a fourteenth state. Such a treaty he had no authority to even propose, let alone conclude. But Hamilton was confident in his support from the still unassailable Washington, and he fretted not a bit about such diplomatic details. He would win over the senate after the fact, and if that Jacobite Virginian squire at the Department of State was offended or outraged, then so be it. The fly in the ointment turned out not to be any concern with Jefferson, but with Spain's insistence that the port of St. Augustine would stay open to the slave trade.

Both Hamilton and Milton were by now both converted to abolition, and Hamilton had secret dreams of adding a state free of the abomination of slavery. In this effort Erasmus would have roundly approved, and the plan was a foreshadowing of an issue that would some day rent their beloved new nation asunder. But the Spanish Crown would not be persuaded.

In a separate parlor, Erasmus had been much more successful. Showing a young, handsome version of the more mature charm to which we were now so familiar, he had won the heart of the beautiful Elena Garza. So by evening's end, two things were clear: Florida would for now remain Spanish, but the lovely Elena Garza would not.

For the balance of his friendship with Erasmus, Alexander Hamilton would say that in the weeks that followed, he was the primary negotiator in the "Treaty of Elena." He, as Erasmus' representative, negotiated with the elder Garza all the important issues of the courtship. To be decided were the issues of Elena's Catholic faith, the church in which the children would be raised, Erasmus' ability to support Elena and her eventual children, and the final term that Erasmus and Elena must agree to reside with Enriquez in Philadelphia until he was recalled to Spain. All issues being thus settled, the couple was married by a local priest in a catholic ceremony at the home of Enriquez Garza on January 6, 1784.

Eventually Erasmus and Elena returned to New York, and it was reported that in keeping with his word, he was for the balance of Elena's life "as good a Papist Catholic as any New England Federalist Anglican could ever hope to be."

The years rolled by, and children followed. An increasing fortune, born of Erasmus' ever more obvious business brilliance, placed the Miltons atop the New York social scene. The passion and affection of their marriage was legendary.

Their life together was marred only by their growing perception that he was not aging at a normal pace. This was a phenomenon that Elena at first enjoyed, then wondered at, and eventually grew to dread. As would any woman, she feared growing older as her husband stayed young and attractive. She aged with grace, yet age is a wicked and heartless foe to the beauty of a young woman. New York's social and business community lost track of this strange process. For the sake of appearances poor Elena had to begin playing the part of a matron, and introducing Erasmus first as her son, and then her grandson, and so on. She suffered greatly, yet stoically and quietly, happy only in the knowledge that her dear husband continued to love her, and had never ceased to care for her.

Erasmus never let the growing difference in age effect his doting affection for her, and he loved her until her death in Albany, New York, at the age of sixty-one, in 1845.

He had her buried beneath a joint monument at their Hudson River estate, and had his name engraved as well on the beautiful memorial stone. From that day on he lived in the hope that some day his curse would be lifted and he could follow her.

Erasmus stoically endured the pain of outliving his children, grandchildren, and great grandchildren. He watched his family spread across the growing nation, until time, distance, and generations caused him to disappear from the collective memory of the Milton clan.

He related to me that once he sat at a Milton family reunion, listening to an old man that was his own great, great grandson. The man was reciting to his grandchildren an old family legend that there was once a Milton who served on Washington's staff, fought at Yorktown with Lafayette, and was the closest confidant of the inventor of our government and the founder of modern markets, Alexander Hamilton. "But such silliness could never be confirmed, as he appears nowhere in the records of the times," the man said. Erasmus never attended another family gathering.

Erasmus never married again, and for quite some time was a somewhat notorious yet matrimonially elusive bachelor on the New York society scene. He attended charity balls given by Hamilton's exquisite sister in law, Angela Church, and contributed vast sums to various and sundry causes.

He was a great benefactor to the widow Eliza Hamilton's charitable efforts on behalf of New York's widows and orphans, and over time made peace with his "odd capacity to not age normally."

"So it is this history that is the well spring of my affection for your family," he concluded. "I assure you I mean no disrespect to your lovely wife, who reminds me of my own dear Elena. I thank God he has again blessed me with a family, and I pray that it will be my last." This last comment struck me as ominous, because both Beda and I had noticed recently that ever since we began the publication of the "Tacitus" essays, Erasmus Milton had begun to age.

His confiding of this story to us, and I think in retrospect perhaps his own recognition of his changing pace of aging, seemed to energize him. The pace of his writing increased, and early the next day another work from "Tacitus" slid through the old mail slot. This particular effort has become a prize possession of my wife, who grew to view the dear old man as a father.

Great Men

I have had in my long life the privilege of knowing many great men. Some revealed greatness in the history of our nation. Certainly included is our beloved Virginia general, who led us in the "Glorious Cause" and invented the institution of the presidency. Surely too was my own beloved friend Hamilton, who invented the institutions that became our blessed Union, and Lincoln, who saved it. T.R. Roosevelt, the great reformer, was a truly great man, as was his later cousin Franklin.

As an abolitionist, I hold those who brought freedom to people of color as among the greatest of men. Frederick Douglas, William Dubois, one of Colby's finest, Elijah Lovejoy, and Martin Luther King were among the nation's greatest of men.

I am proud myself for the part I played as an abolitionist, yet most proud of a later event. During the civil rights movement I led a group of Colby students to the site of the old slave market in St. Augustine, Florida. There we were to attend a rally put on by Dr. King himself. The old slave market had been converted to a small city park, just down the street from my old friend Henry Flagler's hotel, since then converted to the beautiful and historic Flagler College. We marched through this ironic setting, singing hymns with the great grandchildren of southern slaves.

The State of Florida, under pressure from that fine young president, John Kennedy, had promised police protection. At the crescendo of the rally, as Dr. King himself rose to speak, the ring of Florida State troopers disappeared into the side streets of the old city.

In their place there appeared a large group of hooded, menacing, angry men, armed with various and sundry clubs, guns, and batons. They were ringing the small park and cutting off all escape. For nearly an hour we were pummeled by the canes and clubs of those cowardly sons of a dying southern hatred, hiding their black-hearted shame under hoods of white linen. And that day, for the first time since I led my men across the fields of Flanders, I shed blood for the "Glorious Cause". Nothing in my life has made me more proud than to shed it in the presence of such people of courage. In keeping with the belief and instructions of their leader, the brave and noble Dr. King, they offered no resistance. They accepted every blow, and with each injury they awakened the conscience of our great and merciful land. In their being beaten down, our land began to rise up, and in no other way could they have achieved a greater victory. I hold that these marchers were as much patriots in the cause of liberty as the men with whom I served on the fields of Saratoga or in the twisted, smoke-filled forests of Antietam. They took their place with the Founders that day, in service to the "Glorious Cause".

I am equally proud since those tumultuous times of my most beloved country. It is well on its way to completing the task for which so many sacrificed so much in the abolitionist cause. When, for example, I married a woman of color in my youth, I was the subject of quiet gossip in the North and open distain in the South.

My lovely Elena was Catholic, she was Spanish, and she was brown. While her goodness did not shield her from bigotry, it allowed her to persevere. She was full of love, compassion, mercy, forgiveness, fortitude, and courage. She was beautiful in both a physical and spiritual sense. She was humble before God and her husband, but she possessed the fire of Spanish blood and the carriage of nobility that commanded respect. She was a lover beyond comparison, full of passion, yet for her husband alone. In all the years of our life together, I found no fault in her. She was perfect.

Yet there were those who hated her because she was not white. They hated us because of what we proved was possible and because we disproved the validity of their hate. Never did she dwell on the pain this caused her, and like the Christ upon the cross of her ever present crucifix, she forgave all insult as being born only of unenlightened ignorance. "Don't fret so, my dear husband," she would say. "Have you ever known an intelligent bigot? Such a being does not exist, and if he did we would not seek his approval nor need him to confirm us."

Yet I grieved for her that there were places we could not go, and friends that, for their own well-being, were our friends only in private. All this in a land where "all men are created equal."

Yet today, in that same land, I have a literary benefactor who sees now to the publication of my claim to the title of Founding Father. This man has married a replication of my beloved Elena, one so like her that I am sure somewhere in her linage appears the name Garza.

This Mexican immigrant, like the ancestor I have assigned to her, is brown in a white land. Yet I thrill to see that she is a jewel in her local society, revered by her family, loved by her neighbors, and held as a treasure by her community. She goes where she wishes without threat of rebuke, as do her interracial children. Her Christian love blinds even the hardest of bigots to her color, and she converts every life she touches to the modern goals of the heirs of abolition. I find no fault in her.

In the kindest of gestures, my new family early this winter allowed me to accompany them to their family cottage in none other than old St. Augustine. I stood there once more in the old slave market, in the center of this beautiful, enlightened old city. I thought of the activity there, the buying and selling of souls, that had been the undoing of my good friend Hamilton's scheming over two centuries before.

I remembered the shedding of blood there for the cause of civil rights 175 years later. And now, my new family, with their various shades of white, black, and brown, walked freely through the ancient city. Not only need they not fear violence, but they suffered not even a judgmental frown or disapproving glance. My heart leapt with joy as I alone could understand the significance of that simple fact. Would that my fallen abolitionist brother and martyrs to the "Cause" could have seen what I had seen this day, on the grounds of the old slave market.

In my old age I ramble on, having been distracted this day by the gift, through Beda, of the illusion of again spending time with my beloved Elena. But the point of my story is this: It is incumbent upon us as a nation to recognize, cherish, and nurture those things that are good. Equality is good. Charity is good. Work is good. Religion is good. Yet there may be no greater good to society than the coupling of an honorable man to a woman of kindness, charity, and grace, in the creation of a household that we have named "family". It is from this well alone that we draw the souls of great men and women as they are needed across time and generations. Woe indeed to a people who substitute the libertine for liberty, and in the service of removing all restrictions on personal behaviors and social trends come to disparage or neglect that wellspring of good citizens. For without the brick and mortar of what is now termed the "traditional family," the house of true liberty will not withstand the weight of time, and it will fall.

Tacitus

Chapter Eight
Bill of Corrections

Upon our return from St. Augustine in the early winter of 2005, I took Erasmus to a lecture at Ohio Northern. The speaker was Associate Justice Clarence Thomas, and the old abolitionist was excited indeed to hear, in person, a black man who had risen to such a high judicial station. My old friend was a voracious reader of Supreme Court opinions, and admired Thomas for several of his views in particular. "Were the nine justices a set of knives, Thomas would not be the sharpest blade; that title I leave to Scalia," he once said. "But his strong belief in private property and limitations on the 'takings' power is exactly correct. And his understanding of natural law and its role in our thinking at the beginning is fascinatingly accurate. Without that concept, all thoughts of applying the concept of individual liberty from the Bill of Rights to our abolition movement would have had no foundation. Thomas understands that what we did that May of 1787 in Philadelphia was part law, part history, and part mysticism. We balanced the need for order with the longing for liberty, and he has not perverted that balance."

After the speech, we took our normal walk across campus, and I chuckled to myself as Erasmus explained to two young law students about "the difference between personal liberty and acting on every whim of libertine personal indulgence."

I always found it pleasant when students spontaneously gathered, which seemed to happen every time Erasmus would pause to speak. It was obvious that he had become somewhat of a cult celebrity at Ohio Northern, and the students indulged his conservative views much more than they would have an equally conservative professor or peer. The anger and loudness that tends to cohabitate with revolutionary zeal in the breast of young radicals melted away in his presence. He often told the students that he too was a revolutionary, more so than they could know. He told the students that he had bled and would do so again for their right to gather there on the campus green, and encouraged them to "buy and sell their wares in the free market of ideas."

This particular night, with the president recently reelected, a student in the group loudly proclaimed that Bush would ruin the country with his appointments to the high court. Some agreed, but most turned instinctively to the old man, who smiled and replied thus: "Well, young man, thankfully our brilliant libertine from Virginia was in Paris when we met in Philadelphia, so we avoided the disaster of popularly elected justices. Consequently, once our Mr. Bush appoints those whom you so fear, they will no longer be beholden to him, or to you, or to me. They will seek the council of their own mind, of the other justices, hopefully of the law, and of no one else. No justice is ever exactly what his appointer thinks he or she will be, and none has ever been as good as we hoped or as bad as we feared.

So, my dear boy, our president, your president, will not ruin the country. He, like Washington, Lincoln, Truman, and Reagan before him, is a man whose defining trait is not his great intellect, but his great conviction."

Myself, Erasmus, and several older law students then retired to a local student pub called The White Bear Inn (aptly named for the Ohio Northern mascot, the polar bear). There we spent the balance of the night enchanted by stories of the Federalist Papers, Hamilton, Jay, Madison, and the Founders' insights on original constitutional theory. Two hundred years of practice had found Erasmus quite adept at couching his first hand knowledge of such people and events, when in settings where his intimate recollections might make his age become an issue. He justified his knowledge with old, vague, and often concocted historical sources, and he delivered his opinions and facts with such confidence that rarely did anyone question him.

My old friend dozed briefly on the way home from Ada to Lafayette, but must have awakened later that night at home. Perhaps the evening of recollecting the intents of the Founders, of explaining them to the students, and the haunting of old memories and old friends had again interrupted his rest. My poor old friend talked often of how a life so full and extended led often to an excess of dreaming, and that he had difficulty sleeping.

In any case, he must have spent the remainder of the night a slave again to his pen. For the next morning, another essay appeared from the pen of our ancient philosopher.

Bill of Corrections

I admit that at times I took issue with our young Virginian author of liberty. I found his contribution to the "Cause" indispensable, but at the same time I found his smug self-appointment as the final definer of individual freedom unendingly annoying. That said, his Jacobite indulgence of mob rule is long forgiven, and history has proven his Bill of Rights to be the perfect capstone to our miracle enacted in Philadelphia in 1787. His borrowing of the list of ten from God himself (an odd choice given his own strange relationship with that deity) was a perfect format as well. Yet Jefferson's restrictions on the central power have long ago been eroded, whereas Hamilton's "implied powers" have been the defining theory in the subsequent evolving of our constitution.

The nature of this evolution of our constitution has come mostly through the decisions of our Supreme Court, which over time has, in some instances, showed great wisdom, and in others shown an increasing lack of fidelity to the supremacy of law. Hamilton saw this fidelity to law, even those laws with which one disagrees, as our best protection against tyranny. It seems at times our modern justices, however, increasingly succumb to the desire to make history and impact events.

They leave the loving bosom of their spouse the law, and sleep instead with the harlots of personal opinion and public political approval. Without the acceptance of the theory that the Constitution means simply what it says, restraints on the power of government start to give way to the natural desire of the State to tell everyone what they can and cannot do. Thus does tyranny begin to chip away at the roots of the tree of liberty.

To set back this process, and to return our Constitution again to its own purity of purpose and design, I would again draw, as did Jefferson, on God's fascination with a list of ten simple statements of truth. What I propose is to call another gathering of the States, a convention if you will, to consider these ten amendments to our Constitution. I refer to these ten additional amendments as The Bill of Corrections.

Article XXVII: Article I of this Constitution's Bill of Rights shall not be construed as prohibiting federal, state, or local governments from exhibiting religious symbols such as the Ten Commandments, nativity scenes, or other religious symbols. Nor shall it be construed as prohibiting voluntary prayer, or instructions of moral values using religion or religious tradition or text, in public schools, so long as local communities, through their elected officials, consent to these activities.

Article XXVIII: No government may take private property from a private entity or individual and transfer it to another private entity or individual using the concept of eminent domain, or any other power, to enact the public good. Article V shall be construed as granting only the government the right to take and use private property, with payment of compensation, from a private entity or person.

Article XXIX: In that marriage as we know it is a religious institution that has taken upon itself the trappings of civil law, and in that in its civil context the law expands required participation and responsibility beyond the two married persons, this Constitution shall limit the definition of marriage as between a man and a woman having been so naturally born.

Article XXX: This constitution neither prohibits nor guarantees the right of abortion, and leaves the question of its legality, restriction, and regulation to the legislative branch, and should it so assign, to the States.

Article XXXI: This constitution prohibits individual states from taxing interstate commerce, and prohibits states from taxing citizens of other states simply because goods may be shipped across or into said state. Commerce shall be taxed where it is domiciled, and the simple act of shipping goods into or across state lines shall not create such domicile. An individual's wages, pensions, and other income shall be taxed in the state where he or she lives.

Article XXXII: This constitution prohibits any government from outlawing the ownership or use of firearms for personal or protective use. But it does not guarantee the right to own arms reasonably deemed to be suited only for military use, nor does it prohibit reasonable regulation to limit access of criminals to weapons.

Article XXXIII: Article I of this Constitution's Bill of Rights shall not be construed as prohibiting local communities, through their locally elected officials, from prohibiting or regulating the sale, distribution, or transmission of material, performances, or media deemed by them to be pornographic. Interstate media transmission of material to individuals shall continue to be regulated by the central federal authority.

Article XXXIV: No law shall be enacted or construed to prohibit licensed professions from restricting or regulating the content of the advertising of their members through state boards or professional societies, so long as no prohibition exists against publishing the price of service.

Article XXXV: This constitution does not protect the rights of foreign nationals or non-citizens captured committing or conspiring to commit acts of war upon the United States, regardless of their location of capture.

Nor does it protect the rights of U.S. citizens captured in foreign lands in the service of a foreign enemy as a soldier, during periods of time when that foreign enemy is committing or conspiring to commit acts of war against the United States.

Article XXXVI: While the legislature is free to enact those statutes it feels are just for the protection of other parties, the rights and privileges of this Constitution are extended only to citizens of the United States. Nor is this Constitution subservient to any treaty or foreign authority or power as concerns those citizens.

Respectfully submitted for ratification,

Tacitus

Chapter Nine
Lessons in Diplomacy

During the college break during the 2004 holidays, I spent many interesting evenings with Erasmus. Since school was not in session at ONU, he was not able to take the short ride to Ada from his home in Lafayette to pester the students there with his much loved informal lectures. One evening we were drinking wine, as we often did, and discussing my newest addition to my "smart room" library. It was an interesting history of slavery in America by James and Lois Horton. The wine was a pleasant cabernet from a small winery in northeast Ohio, the Marco Vineyards. Erasmus had provided the intelligence on this small vineyard, and he maintained it was the only Ohio wine that could stand with the old Spanish California family vineyards, or his own Hudson Valley and New York Erie Coast holdings. I was again reminded by this conversation that a talented man who had multiple lifetimes at his disposal could become very wealthy indeed. I was the benefactor in this small way, as he ordered Marco wine by the case, and we sampled it often.

As our conversations drifted back to the new book, it came as no surprise to me that he had already read and developed opinions about it. As he expressed these opinions as they related to his own experiences during the late slavery period, I began to realize that he had a much greater role in the Lincoln war rooms than he had previously divulged. As a student of history greatly interested in the slavery and abolition period, I pressed further.

It seems that my friend Erasmus was somewhat of an ostracized radical in his early days at the Lincoln War Department. He spent almost all his time aggressively advocating from the outset of the war for the abolition of slavery and the raising of free black regiments for service to the Union. He did so at times to the neglect of his other duties, so much so that he was twice demoted, and often sent back to central Maine on meaningless missions as a liaison to the abolitionists who met there. On these missions he would go once again, as he did at Hamilton's murder, to the intellectual confines of beautiful Colby College. There he would repine with his abolitionist friends, rest his mind and soul on the banks of the Kennebec, and let the mountains of Maine absorb and mend the constant sadness brought on by thoughts of long past friends and loved ones. It was here, time and again, that in his strange state of agelessness he came to avoid madness. Lincoln, meanwhile, would gain some much needed respite from Erasmus' constant harping on the issues of black freedom and black soldiers.

It was during one of these trips to New England that Erasmus met the famous Underground Railroad heroine Harriet Tubman. There he learned of her plans to return to the recently captured Sea Island plantations on the Carolina coast for the purpose of organizing contraband slaves into military units and commando scouts for the Union army. Erasmus contributed heavily to her fundraising and joined her traveling party.

Lincoln, gradually warming to the idea of fighting men of color, had a great need for soldiers and a lessening fear of offending border states. Consequently he endorsed the mission, and made Erasmus' role official. He was now a special covert liaison to the efforts to put freed slaves and free northern blacks in the field.

In this capacity, Erasmus befriended Robert Gould Shaw of the 54th Massachusetts (United States Colored Troops). His experience in training and commanding non-traditional recruits, which he had garnered training minutemen and New York militia during the Revolution, made him a valuable addition to Shaw's staff.

In an ironic twist of fate, Erasmus again saw action storming a coastal redoubt at Fort Wagner, charging a Carolina fortress with a close young friend at his side. This reprise of an earlier battle must have seemed to him some strange form of déjà vu. As he charged Fort Wagner with Colonel Shaw at his side, he no doubt thought of his friend the Marquise de Lafayette, an early convert to the anti-slavery ranks, who was by his side years earlier in a previous war, as they faced British fire at Yorktown. Yet Lafayette, Hamilton, and Milton, the three dashing young officers of Washington's staff, all survived the storming of Yorktown. At the end of this day, Colonel Robert Gould Shaw and a full one third of his young, brave, black soldiers lay dead in the sand at the base of the walls of Fort Wagner.

Erasmus, with three bullet holes in his coat, a wounded arm, and a re-aggravated wound to his leg first suffered at Saratoga, was later decorated for regrouping the assault force, holding his position until nightfall, and leading the remnants of the 54'Th Massachusetts to safety in a daring nighttime withdraw under fire.

Erasmus was despondent over Shaw's death at Fort Wagner, likening it to the loss of his beloved friend Hamilton. He viewed it his duty to carry on the love for the free black soldiers of the 54[th,] so nobly shown by the gallant Colonel Shaw, and he financially aided veterans of that unit and their families for the remainder of their lives.

After Shaw's death, Erasmus returned for a while to his place of solace at Waterville, prayed again at the Colby College chapel, and found once more the courage to go on. He returned to Washington, and gained permission to use his and his Hudson

Valley supporters' private funds to raise, equip, and command the only cavalry unit in the United States Colored Troops. He commanded this unit, the 12th Regiment, U.S. Mounted Volunteers, until the end of the war.

I felt a deep sadness for my old friend, the more I became aware of the absolute loneliness that was part of the burden of this strange extended life span. His physical fatigue was becoming more apparent, but his emotional burdens required great discipline to not evolve into despair.

He had, in his long life, lost Hamilton, his mentor, to a duelist's bullet; Shaw, his friend, to a rebel's cannonade; and Elena, his love, to the march of time. Until his discovery of this small town in northwest Ohio, it seemed that Colby College, on the banks of the Kennebec River, in his rustic adopted Maine, was the only place where peace could come to conquer his grief.

This evening was somewhat emotionally draining for my dear old friend, and it was several days before the most recently recruited student delivered the newest essay, sliding it early in the morning through the mail slot in my door. The timing of the delivery made it apparent that my old friend had again found sleep difficult, and had no doubt written though the night.

PEACE

I often wondered how our founding Virginian General could so clearly understand the minds of nations, while our other brilliant Virginian Founder spent his life drifting aimlessly as if lost through the fog of moral intents and good intentions.

My dear General Washington held no illusions. All nations act in their own self-interest, and he thought agreements between nations that were based only on the desire to "do good," without the inclusion of mutual self-interest, were doomed.

Hence he concluded the Jay Treaty, and guided the nation away from the French Jacobins. War with England at the time, while construed as the holy pursuit of democracy and freedom, served the interest of revolutionary France, not America.

Poor Jefferson, however, would have committed our young nation to another war with England, in order to aid the chaotic "liberty" of the French revolution.

I have found over the span of my oddly extended life that idealists seeking peace are a dangerous lot. They view peace as some sort of deity to be worshipped or destination to be reached. Their influence on our public policy has often left us unprepared, and many a tyrant or bully has been tempted into conflict with us by the appearance of a lack of resolve created by these pacifist innocents.

Lincoln, like Washington, understood that the greater good must synergize with the good of the nation. Against what my sense of justice was at the time, Lincoln first delayed the freeing of the slaves, acting as he did to save the Union. This was a recognition of national self-interest. Yet he ended slavery and ultimately pursued justice, as good nations should. He acted then, when both the service of justice and the good of the nation could be satisfied.

My point is this: Good nations, prepared for war and willing to smite evil with a mighty hand, will prevent many a conflict before it starts. But the leap to war must never be for the sake of smiting evil alone. There is always evil, and perpetual war is no way to fight it. So for good nations to take up arms, they must know that not only is evil smitten, but the ultimate good of the nation is served.

Justice and democracy should always be sown in the furrow left by the cold steel plow blade of war. If you do so, then your army will never again revisit that field. For where freedom, justice, and the basic rights of man are growing, there you will find peace. But the nation's arms should not be committed for the good of others alone. It must also serve our own vital interests. Hence the "Glorious Cause" was fought to establish our nation and to achieve freedom and liberty. The great Civil War was fought to save the Union and to free the slaves. Fighting tyrants from Hitler to Hussein was done not just to remove them from harming others, but to keep them from harming us.

To insist on such a duality of interests is to set a high bar. But a review of our history and of study of our conflicts teaches us that when this test is not applied, we either act beneath the standards of our calling, or we fail in our endeavor.

Tacitus

Chapter Ten
A Respectful Dissent

It is little wonder that my dear old Erasmus had little tolerance for those who would suggest that the government had a moral duty to care for those who chose not to even try to care for themselves. My suggestion that our government taught people to expect paternalistic handouts from the government dole from the mid-sixties until the Reagan era fell on deaf ears. I told him that poverty became generational and social mobility ended when Johnson and his Great Society addicted succeeding generations to welfare, and it would take at least that long to reeducate people to rely again on their own effort and skill.

"Immigrant families work menial jobs to educate their children, and those same children go to college and become people of wealth, substance, and significance," he would retort. "The real problem is that government no longer wants people to be self-reliant. Government today is the benevolent slaveholder, living in the big house on the hill. His slaves are fed well with government largess, and are well cared for. But they are still slaves, and they sell their votes to the highest bidder. Were they self-reliant, seeing welfare as a stain on their standing as free and successful citizens, they would be independent and hard to control. They would vote for the person who would best serve the Republic, not the person who would protect their Social Security, free drug benefits, food stamps, or rent subsidy."

It is hard to respond to someone who speaks the truth but speaks it harshly. I have long believed that government seeks to control through largess, and is not nearly as caring as it pretends to be. Our cultural decay and the creation of perpetual cross-generational poverty clearly shows the failure and harm of government welfare programs. They have done so much more harm than good that it can hardly be measured. But stating the truth clearly, with an open confidence in the style of a Founding Father, would surely open up my old friend to the tired old liberal argument of not caring about the poor. Not that he ever cared about the accusations of those he would merely dismiss as "Jacobins and Jeffersonians."

Erasmus cared even less for those citizens who populated what we now call the Peace Movement. Given that he served in combat in every war from our revolution through the Spanish American war, and served in governmental roles in all subsequent war efforts, it is no surprise that he held such people in utter contempt.

On a brief break from classes in March of 2005, Erasmus traveled with Beda and I to New York. He had it in his mind that I must fully understand his contribution as a Founder. And to do so, I must understand that the Founding Father's work did not end with the Revolution. It extended on to the building of the nation. Hence we were off to New York, where he could explain his role with Hamilton in the founding of the stock markets and the creation of the National Bank.

As we walked toward the Wall Street exchange building, across from the famous statue of the huge bull, we came upon a group of war protestors, exactly of the ilk that would cause Erasmus to lose his temper. He did not disappoint. One of the protestors approached us with a pamphlet. He was about the age of the students that regularly greeted Erasmus back on campus in Ada, but he lacked any of the reverence and affection those young people held for the old man. This poor unfortunate boy had the misfortune to confront the old warrior, who having once braved British steel to stride victorious on a Yorktown redoubt, saw nothing to fear from this shouting youth.

"Would you give your son's life to pacify Najif?" the boy screamed at Erasmus. "Would you let your child die for Iraqi oil? Stop the war now!"

Erasmus, old as he was, moved like a cat to confront the young protestor, drawing up with all the indignation he could muster not inches from the young man's face. "Am I to understand, sir, that you rally support here against our own boys while they are in the field? What say you, man? I would call you a coward, but a coward must know and understand bravery and duty, then fail in his calling out of a concern for the safety of his own pathetic ass. You, sir, understand nothing. You are a copperhead of the worst sort, claiming the moral high ground as a lover of peace, when in truth you are a hater of your own good land."

I thought Erasmus was done, as the boy stepped back, stunned by the energy of the old man. But he raised his voice to a thunder and continued. "Were our Republic to free every soul on earth, you would find some fault in our motives. Would your own country feed every hungry child or slay every tyrant, you would find some error or injustice in our methods. Give my son's life, you ask? If indeed I had endured such a loss and then I was confronted by you, sir, I would cane-whip your hide until you crawled back to whatever brood has crammed your head with such drivel. How dare you use such sacrifice to advance your own Tory agenda. Debate if you must the choice to go to war, sir, but once our boys are facing shot and steel, then keep your peace. Now step aside, sir, before I decide to strike a blow for those unfortunate ones who have indeed lost boys to the Cause!"

Needless to say, the poor boy was speechless. Those of a liberal bent seem to feel that they have some inalienable right to hold the moral high ground unchallenged in all public debate.

And when they are laid low, as this young protestor unexpectedly was, they oft times find themselves speechless and befuddled. So step aside he did, to my great relief, acting at least for the moment like a real pacifist. Erasmus, to the cheers of several dozen bystanders, stood boldly on the Wall Street sidewalk like a knight having just taken the field.

With a grin he pointed out a spot at 68 Wall Street where there once stood an old Buttonwood tree. He proceeded then to tell us a fascinating story about how, in its shade, he, Hamilton, and several other gentlemen had conducted the first meeting of the New York Stock Exchange.

When we returned to Lafayette, it was only a few days before Tacitus again drew his pen.

A Respectful Dissent From the Premise Peace Movement

It has often been publicly argued by members of the Peace Movement that their movement is Christian, and those who oppose them are less Christian for having done so.

I believe that Christians have a biblically imposed duty to aid, assist, and, when necessary, defend the defenseless when they are harmed by a clearly evil force. When nations are themselves threatened by such a force, this duty applies as well to them.

I believe that the dictator of Iraq, having visited unspeakable horrors on his own people and those nations around him, is such an evil force.

I believe the American Peace Movement, in the days leading to war, gave the appearance to this dictator of an uncommitted and divided nation.

During this period, much effort was being directed toward him to cease his evil and abandon his post. The appearance of a divided nation created by the Peace Movement contributed to his decision to seek war instead of accommodation. I believe this movement should address its unintended effect of assisting this evil dictator in his efforts to stay in power.

I believe the American Peace Movement has, in this instance, sacrificed freedom, justice, liberty, and the elimination of tyranny and torture in their pursuit of an unconditional peace. In doing so they are abandoning the victims of Saddam. Consequently, the blood of these victims is on their hands, in the same sense that the blood of the Holocaust is on the hands of the German Catholic and Lutheran churches of the 1930s.

I believe that the Peace Movement believes there is no evil worse than war. I also believe when they say things like "We support the troops, but not the war," and "We believe in victory without war," that they are watering down their real beliefs to make them more politically tenable. I also believe they are wrong. There are evils worse than war.

I believe that honest and sincere Christians can disagree with the notion that pacifism is an appropriate and implementable national policy. I believe that honest and sincere Christians can believe that there are greater evils than war, and that there is such a thing as a justifiable war.

I understand that a great public debate is a healthy thing before committing the nation to war, and that I may indeed be wrong in thinking that now is such a time to make such a commitment. Yet I greatly resent the implication that to believe such things makes me less of a Christian that a peace activist.

I believe that peace is not an object to be possessed, but instead is a state of being between nations that is achieved with the establishment of sound policies. When the elimination of tyranny, the establishment of justice under law, the right of private property and self-determination, and the spread of democracy are the object of successful policy, then peace develops as a consequence. Thus it is the defenders of justice and liberty who are the peacemakers, for they are pursuing real peace.

Tacitus

Chapter Eleven
We Will Remember Them

Upon returning from New York, Erasmus fell ill. I sat with him daily after teaching my class at ONU, and conveyed to him the best wishes of the young students with whom he loved to spar. He mentioned often how odd it seemed to be ill, as he had not been so since before the death of his friend Hamilton. Normally when one is ill, he is a somewhat helpless and at times childlike creature. Erasmus, on the other hand, was fascinated with his illness and its impact on his body. His lungs were less efficient, so he had to know why. His hands, always strong and young, had begun to show signs of wrinkles, and he studied his skin with a strange abstraction. He had no fear of not recovering. He had completely internalized the faith of his Elena, an absolute conviction that at the moment of his death he would see her again, and it was obvious from his life's history that he had no fear of death.

It was during this time that Erasmus divulged some of his most personal remembrances. We talked of Washington's grief at the sense of betrayal he felt when Jefferson aided his political enemies. He talked of how as Lafayette languished in prison, the old General suffered at having to put the interests of his country beyond his personal desire to send aid to his young

69

French protégé'. He told me of he and Hamilton's wild days at King's College, and how they shoved the Tory president of the school out a back window, saving him from a gathering mob of revolutionary students and townspeople.

He wept recalling the illness and death of his beloved Elena, who was sixty-two at her death. I wept with him, many times, as he related the anguish he concealed from his beloved, as he tried to look older, and she struggled to remain his beautiful young bride. I came to see with him, that age is a mild and subtle poison that comes painlessly upon you if it is shared with the love of your life. But to face it alone is a cold and lonely curse indeed. He had cursed his body then for not growing old with her, and he blamed his desire for glory and recognition for cursing him to face abandoning her at her death. At her passing he fell again into a depression that sent him scurrying once more to the central mountains of his adopted Maine.

My beloved old philosopher took me, during that winter, from the surrender at Yorktown to his service with Lincoln.

Together we led cavalry charges with his beloved black buffalo soldiers of the 12th New York, and we braved again the gas in the Argonne forest. He showed me such letters, from such men and women of history, that it would take a lifetime to relate them all.

I feared that wet and chilly spring that I was losing my dear old friend. I had begun, as you know, to notice that he was finally aging. I now knew that it was I who was the cause, and many nights I vowed to demand that he write no more. I wanted to keep forever this old and dear friend, who loved my wife and children, who loved my little college, and who I now realized loved me like a son.

Like he, I blamed my desire for recognition, this human stain of pride, for having started him down the road to writing his essays. But during these cold winter nights in his parlor, surrounded by what to me were artifacts, but to him were mementos of his life, he convinced me that all was finally as it should be.

"Remember in New York," he said one evening. "Remember how roughly I treated that young boy? He was, granted, a know-nothing young scallywag, but he was sincere. I had no right to berate him so. It was for him that I first took up my sword in the "Cause", so he could stand on the street and speak his mind. Later that week when I stood at "Ground Zero", I shook with tears. It wasn't just the grief for the fallen, but for myself. I'm getting old, my dear friend. These are no longer my times. When I offer my sword now, no one takes it up. When I heard this young man Bush was sending young firebrands to export our freedom and slay the bastards that spawned this fascist form of Islam, I was ecstatic.

I assembled my resume of service, and copied the commissions I have held in the beloved Republic's service for every war from the "Glorious Cause" to World War II. I cleaned my revolver, donned my uniform, and looked in the mirror to see that all was ready. And this old man, this shadow of me, looked back into my eyes and told me, 'Not this battle, old man. Not this time.' So I put my commissions away and sought out this place. It is here, in this little town, named for my brother in arms at Yorktown, that I found salvation, my friend. For it is here that I found you."

"If I publish what you write, then you will die, and it will be on me," I said.

"Don't kill me off quite so fast," he said with a grin. "I'm just getting old, I'm not hanging myself. I'm no cowardly bastard like that old crow Burr, damn his soul. I'll stay around long enough for you to see that I take my place with the other Founders, like you promised. I'll not have spent all those years chanting rosaries in Spanish to make sure I get into heaven, and then when I get there have no stories of my own to tell. Washington will tell stories about his war, and Hamilton about his bank. And I, what shall I do? By God, I'll sit at the Founder's table, with Elena sitting at my side, and I will tell of my friend the professor, and how he saved my memory by the publication of my federalist essays. If the history books insist on ignoring me, then you will see to it that I get my due. Then I'll die, my friend, and not a day too soon. But if I stop writing, dear sir, and you stop publishing, then I will surely be dead forever."

We said nothing else that evening, but just looked at the fire and enjoyed being together. The next visit, he handed me an envelope, and in it was the next essay from our illustrious Tacitus

Courage

My old friend Hamilton was not above berating his nemesis Mr. Jefferson for his failure to serve under arms during the fighting for our "Glorious Cause". At the time I concurred with Alexander's assessment, but as I age I think perhaps we were misplacing our animosity. The brilliant Virginian had a role to play, assigned by God, in this great play whose purpose it was to create this land. And in retrospect, I admit he played it well. I begrudge him not the warm fire of his home hearth while we froze in the huts of Valley Forge, nor his safety in his parlor while we took shot and ball and bled the ground red at Saratoga.

As we are again at war, I think again of those who fell. I remember the great president Ronald Reagan, who stood weeping in an airplane hanger while the bodies of young marines were brought in to lie in state. Looking over the caskets draped in the flag of the "Glorious Cause", I remember his breaking voice: "Where," he asked, "where do we get such men?"

I have asked that question many times. What love of country or will of iron drives a man to wrap his feet in cloth and stay bootless in the snow, when others desert and go home? What inner voice tells a man to not break ranks when his comrades fall around him? What bravery causes a man to stay at his gun while his ship rolls over and entombs him in the sea? What mission pushes a man up the steps of a burning tower while others flee down the same stairs?

I do not know the answer. From Valley Forge to Gettysburg, from Pearl Harbor to the Twin Towers, I know only that our country has always had such men. I know this to be a fact. Above all else that I have done in this life, I am most honored to have served with those who have braved great danger in service of a country that has called them to duty. Those who have never been called to such duty, even if they do all they can in support of our men at arms, look deep into their own souls and find themselves unworthy of the same praise as those who served. They forever find themselves wanting, perhaps by no fault of their own, but wanting nonetheless.

Must a man spill his blood or risk his life to call himself a patriot? I would make no such claim. Jefferson raised no sword and risked no limb on any field, and he was indeed a patriot. But to those who have, to those who gave battle in our name in any war, however history judged the endeavor, it is they who have earned eternal praise, eternal gratitude, from all the sons and daughters of Liberty.

Courage is a fleeting moment when fear is overcome by the bitter stew of discipline and duty. In the eyes of those who have proven they posses it, there is an understanding, a knowing that no one else can fully understand. Where do we get such men? In retrospect, it is a question we cannot answer. It is enough that we promise them, those who have fallen, that we will eternally guard that for which they fell, and we will remember them.

Tacitus

Chapter Twelve
Watergate Escalation

It was now April of 2005, and I had known my dear Erasmus for nearly a year. Winter term had finished at little Ohio Northern. Erasmus was again well, and he resumed his daily walks at the campus. I myself had more time to write, to work with the paper, and to spend with him, so I took advantage.

We scheduled a time to sit in the quiet of the campus law library conference room, where Erasmus had agreed to undergo a formal historical interview. I was quite excited, and spent quite a bit of time developing a list of questions. I knew this was part of Erasmus' payment to me for publishing his "Tacitus" essays, and I wanted to fully utilize this opportunity while he was in a non-combative mood.

His answers were sometimes terse, but I was amazed at his ability to recollect details and facts specific to any subject matter. And not only facts, but also at his age to so confidently hold opinions and express them so concisely on demand. You will understand my meaning when you read this sample of my list of questions, and his sometimes humorous and always interesting responses.

Q: Who was our best president?

A: Best? I would say Washington. He invented the office. All the others that I would consider "great" later built on his example, and learned from it. He painted on a blank canvas. Like Hamilton invented the federal government, Washington invented the presidency.

Q: Who would you say was the greatest president of the nineteenth century?

A: Greatest? Is greatest different than best? Jefferson had his moments, yet like so many others he governed like those whom he had earlier opposed. This great enemy of central government authority advanced it more than perhaps any other, save Lincoln. Monroe had his "doctrine", but we all believed we should separate the new world from the old. I would say Lincoln. Never has a man of so few apparent gifts risen to such genius. He understood politics, public opinion, and people. He was able to be a realist and a populist leader, and still keep his mission in focus and his message on point. Only the later Roosevelt and Reagan captured this same ability. Yes, I would say Lincoln.

Q: And the twentieth century?

A: Here I must declare a draw. I strongly feel the two greatest presidents of the twentieth century were Franklin Roosevelt and Ronald Reagan. You see, the world began again with our glorious revolution. The "Glorious Cause" reestablished liberty and the three great rights of man. For two thousand years, freedom of religion, freedom of speech and self-government, and the right to one's own property and self-improvement— those rights lay dormant. But we awakened them. And when we did, they became the target of great evils.

Just as the simple goodness of Jesus drew the ire of evil and hostile men, so did liberty draw the ire of tyranny, oppression, and dictatorship. In the time of Roosevelt these three great evils took the form of fascist nationalism, and Roosevelt defeated it. Even before fascism, the boil of communism, murderer of half a billion people, festered on the earth. And Reagan defeated it. Both men were great leaders. Both men altered domestic government for the better. Both men defeated great evils.

(Here I interjected an unplanned question)

Q: What do you think of our current president?

A: Real leaders hold real beliefs, and hold steady to them. On that count, this man Bush grades out well. Real leaders are courageous, and understand the great axiom of Lincoln that if you win, your critics won't matter, and if you lose, neither will your good intentions. On this count he also passes. Domestically he has enhanced the right of private property by lowering the abusive takings of taxes. But he has increased dependence with blatant vote buying, so here his grade is mixed. Unlike some, such as Wilson or Carter, he seems to understand evil. You see, evil is amazingly consistent. It wants to exploit, oppress, and harm for the simple sake of doing so. Evil rides many horses and gives them different names. But governmental evil is always the same. It seeks to control the people, at all levels, and in every way. Its name changes, but it is always the same. When evil used nationalism and militarism, it rode a horse called National Socialism. Roosevelt defeated this evil, and filled the void with democracy.

When evil used internal terror and central control, murdering five hundred million people and taking the world to the edge of extinction, it rode a horse called Communism. Reagan defeated this evil and filled the void with democracy.

Now evil has chosen a new method to kill, maim, control, and tyrannize, that being a mutant form of radical religion. This horse's name has again changed, now being called "Radical Islam". Evil once again is riding into town on a different horse, but once again it is the same. Bush is the new sheriff, and he seeks to defeat it and fill the void with democracy. If he succeeds, or sets us on a path where later presidents can, he will have done a great thing. If he does not, then he will be a Truman, a man with great conviction who underachieved.

Q: Who are the greatest men to have never been president?

A: Alexander Hamilton. He invented the structures that are the United States of America. John Marshall. He established the constitution as law. Benjamin Franklin. He was the first great American. Frederick Douglass. He began the process of freeing the slaves. Martin Luther King, Jr. He completed the process of freeing the slaves. Hubert Humphrey. His belief was that every person has the duty to work and should be afforded the opportunity to do so. His belief that workfare is the best welfare is now mainstream thought, and, if adhered to, it may yet reverse the damage wrought by the welfare state. I personally think Jean Kirkpatrick would have made an outstanding president, and I wish John Kennedy could have finished his terms. I'm sure there are others, but I am old.

Q: And the greatest scoundrels?

A: As to the greatest, that is an easy answer. It was Arnold. Had I known his ultimate plan to betray the "Cause", I would have risen from my hospital cot at Saratoga and put a ball in his brain.

Of course there was Burr. Need I further expand on my contempt for this hideous and treasonous murderer of my dear Hamilton? He never did anything, save for himself. He was always scheming, looking to advance his own reputation and status. The "Cause" to him was a vehicle to use as a tool of advancement. His true colors shown forth before it all ended. He was a traitor, and in many ways the first breed of selfish politician. He was a close second to Arnold, to be sure.

Then there was McClellan. How could this pompous little copperhead serve Lincoln so poorly, then try to unseat him in '64? Seeing this little man riding around Washington in his uniform with that silly feather in his hat was truly nauseating. I swear, Jefferson fought harder, and Jefferson never fought at all!

I reserve special contempt for Bedford Forrest. He murdered good black soldiers at Fort Pillow, and founded the KKK. He violated his parole, and had President Grant accepted my recommendation we would have hung him after the war.

I think perhaps a good example of a modern scoundrel is Ramsey Clark, a traitor to his country in every war from Vietnam to the Second Gulf. He was a failure himself in every attempt to serve the "Cause", and holds himself in such high esteem that he apparently feels it is his country, not himself, that is fatally flawed. I don't believe in duels, but if such events were still macaroni, for him I would make an exception.

There were lesser scoundrels, not totally without merit in their own way, such as Harding, Nixon, Johnson, Clinton, and the like. I tend to look more kindly on poor Clinton, whose flaws were personal. He served his country well in his public role, and was a better than average president. In fairness to him, I suppose had I done such things with other women, I would have lied too. The wrath of my beloved Elena would have burned so hot that impeachment would have been a small price to avoid it. Perhaps it was so with Clinton.

In any case, these were not "great" scoundrels, so they do not deserve further mention.

Q: What is the state of politics today?

A: Not nearly as bad as you think. You should take the time to read the exchanges between the newspaper henchmen employed secretly by Hamilton and Jefferson to attack one another, and later by Jefferson to unforgivably attack the old General. We don't even approach the personal cruelty and pure dishonesty employed by those "journalists". We will if things continue to escalate, but we don't yet. God save us from that.

We had talked for some time, and the old boy was getting tired. I took him home, and as he napped in the big reading chair in his magnificent library I spent another wonderful afternoon rummaging through his attic.

As I was leaving, he stirred, and I looked in at him as he slept. He had aged so over our short time together, and he was now old. His once magnificent black pony tail was grey. His face, still distinguished, was now wrinkled. A half full glass of sherry, probably some gift from his old drinking friend Franklin, was sitting on the table beside his wrinkled hand. A sharp stab of guilt pierced my heart once more, and I had to remind myself again that this path he had chosen was taking him where he wanted to go. Back to his friends, back to his time, back to his beloved Elena.

He must have awakened after I left, and the questions and answers of the day had stirred him to write again. The next day a young student, this time a pretty coed who Erasmus had no doubt flirtatiously convinced to go on this "important mission", walked up the steps of my porch and slipped another envelope through the mail slot.

Watergate Escalation

All adults who were once children remember the game of practical jokes called "Gotcha". One child would slightly harm or more likely embarrass the other, who would later retaliate with a slightly greater embarrassment or insult. Further retaliation ensued, after which another, then another, until an adult intervened and the chain was broken.

Thus is the state of American politics today. The Democrats got Nixon, caught him trying to fix an election. So the Republicans got Carter, attacking every aide they could possibly embarrass. Then the Democrats tried to get Reagan, and failed, but they got North, Casey, and whoever else they could. The Republicans then got Clinton, and now the Democrats are after Bush.

Scandal after scandal, with a repetitive game that has simple but destructive rules: First create public embarrassment through an exaggerated or fabricated public scandal. Then subpoena everyone you can, and ask them about everything imaginable in great detail.

Then analyze their testimony and, ignoring the original fabricated scandal, indict them for perjury or obstruction. Gotcha!

The problem is that the concept of "loyal opposition" has been lost in this syndrome that I call Watergate Escalation. The party out of power now does things like employ party operatives to follow people around and listen on their cell phones. They have hit lists for scandal creation and the indictment game, and target anyone who has policy ideas that disagree with their core beliefs. They have bounties for exposing each other's personal flaws, sins, and various and sundry debaucheries. Watergate Escalation is drowning out debate on the issues. No one talks about data, facts, or policy. Everyone just screams about meaningless drivel and scandal, and the hatred spewed at anyone who disagrees with the screaming is simply frightening.

Were it within my power to do so, I would call a secret summit of Democrats and Republicans. This group would decide that it is time for the adults to intervene and put an end to this game of "Gotcha". An agreement should be reached to stop the special investigations, subpoena games, and scandal wars. From now on, only real crimes, in the real sense, will be pursued.

Each side has now impeached a president, each side has ruined lives, and each side has poisoned the tone of the national debate. So let us get the children once more under control, and return to the exchange of ideas and debate based on the merits of policy. Ladies and gentlemen, the republic is 230 years old. It is high time we grew up.

Tacitus

Chapter Thirteen
So Easy To Love

The historical interview format worked wonderfully for me, but my dear old friend quickly tired of it. He exacted a heavy price for its continuance through the balance of April. This price exposed a fondness that my old friend had for the young. He clearly preferred the company of young people to any other, as if from their energy he drew strength of his own. He invariably scoffed at older people who predicted gloom and doom for our society because of the intransigence of any current crop of young people. It is here that his cross generational experience was so valuable. He had a perspective that allowed him to realize that seldom are things as dark as they appear, or as serious as we invariably took them to be.

To continue my interview process, I had to agree to move the interview to the lecture hall at ONU and include his student friends. In addition, I had to agree that questions about current issues must be allowed, and that the sessions be considered a lecture series so his young protégé's could receive some class credit.

Finally, and ominously I thought at the time, he said that before the fall term he must once more visit his home region and walk again on the banks of the Hudson. By this he surely meant that he wished to visit the grave of his beloved Elena.

He said as well that he must pray a final time at the Lorimer Chapel on Mayflower Hill, high above the rolling Kennebec River. He wished once more to find peace where he had always found it, in central Maine, at Colby.

Looking back now, I can see he knew the end was near. We had only a few chapters of his essays to complete, and we both had long ago noted the correlation between his resumed aging and our progress on his federalist papers. He seemed happier and more animated the more he realized that he would soon drink wine again with his long passed friends, see again those with whom he served the "Glorious Cause", and, most of all, return to the arms of his beloved Elena.

"I have kept her waiting longer than a gentleman should," he said, "but I have prayed her beads and said her Hail Mary's as I promised I would. I have clung, as Hamilton advised, to the simple faith of Luther and the rigid rules of the Presbyteries. So when you close my book, dear boy, I will close my eyes and fly to her. I will kiss her little brown hand, and she will curtsey and nod as ladies once did. Grace exchanged for gallantry. So to our pens, good man. We've students waiting and my founding legacy to secure."

Astoundingly, sixty-three students made room in their busy spring class schedules to make sure they could attend the forum hosted by their dear old friend.

Erasmus sat in front of the hall, dressed as a colonial gentleman. He continually tapped his ever present cane, adorned as it was on its tip with a beautiful silver eagle. The students were excited to see Erasmus there, and happier still that he was able to arrange this formal gathering. I could tell from their exchanged glances that the easy credit was a conspiracy between him and his charges to which I had fallen victim. As everyone was seated, I called the group to order and began the class with an introduction;

"My dear friend Erasmus Milton, who you all have come to know, has agreed to play the role of a Founding Father. He will act as if he has lived from then to now. You may ask him anything you like. The rules include that you may ask him about current events as well as historical ones. You may debate him if you dare, but if you rile him I will not protect you. Be prepared to defend your ideas. Now let us begin."

I cannot adequately recreate the scene that took place in that hall in little Ada, Ohio, over the next two weeks. Nor can I reproduce for you all the questions, although a sample is reproduced below. Suffice it to say Erasmus was in wonderful form and spirits. He coaxed the students into debate, challenged them as only the truly wise can, and they were totally enthralled.

Here are, for example, some questions of the students, and his replies:

Q: You helped to found America. Do you now feel, looking back over 200 years, that America has been a force for good in the world? With all our shortcomings, our pollution, our wars, etc., have we really made the world a better place?

A: My dear boy, are you in fact daft? Jefferson even in his most apologetic and anti-federalist moments never doubted that it was our "Glorious Cause" that resurrected the rights of man, entombed as they were beneath the granite ruins of ancient Greece for two thousand years. Life, liberty, property? The power of the government is derived from the consent of the governed? All men are created equal? The Constitution, the Bill of Rights? One must go to Jesus and the eleven to find a group of men who have more impacted the world for good than the Founders of this nation.

And history since then? Who do you think, young man, would have stopped that mad little Austrian corporal? The French? Who would have defeated the murderous Stalinists and put an end to their slaughter of a half billion souls? Estonia? Jesus Christ, Professor, teach ye no history in this institution?

Next question.

Q: We are told by our elders that we are less moral and more spoiled, a generation less worthy. Do you agree?

A: Well, so said Socrates, and here we all are. Less moral? I guess you make less pretence of hiding your sin, and more excuses for it. But I doubt that you actually do it any more than we did. Young women today seem to make a bigger show of what's in their knickers. In the times of my youth, before committing my troth to my beautiful Elena, I do not recall any young girl purposely exposing her under things by wearing low cut blouses, nor did they let the tops of their delicates pop out the back of a pair of boys' dungarees. Yet we seemed to find the target, just the same, and they seemed to help our aim when they wanted to.

Q: What about homosexuality?

A: Young lady, I dare say that this deviance has always been with us. Now note there is no need for you all to go off protesting my speech, nor should you go about drawing erotic pictures on the school sidewalks like the students do at my beloved Colby. I do not use the word "deviance" in its insulting sense, nor do I mean to begrudge anyone their private desires or amusements. I mean merely that a man sheathing his dagger in places intended for other purposes is indeed outside the norm. I do say that society today does seem to spend an inordinate amount of time trying to define the abnormal as normal, and to bring those things that ought to remain private into public forums.

I myself take little note of who or what a person likes to have sex with when I interact with him on a day to day basis. I find it none of my business.

That being said, his unusual tastes do not entitle him to some status under law outside of its normal protections. Nor should a business man be saddled with the cost of insurance and benefits for some unrelated party simple because that party is sharing this deviation with a man in his employ.

And no, before you ask, it is not the same as marriage. Remember, Madame, marriage is not a creation of civil law. Civil law came late to that game. Marriage is the creation of religion, and hence it is religion that may limit marriage to the bonding of men and women.

Q: Is there a "just war"?
A: Yes.

Q: That is it? Just yes?
A: What would you have me say? Have you driven a sword into the chest of another man—a man that no doubt has a wife, perhaps children, a man who serves his country and his cause, even when we see that same cause as an absolute evil? I have done so, and left his body on the field as I moved forward to the next.

Have you given orders knowing that their enactment will cause friends to die, then held those friends in your arms as their blood soaks your tunic and their eyes close for the last time? Again, I have done so.

These are horrible things, evil things. Would you have me say that war is good? Then I would have to endure your uninformed rant about its evilness. Of course it is evil. But history is the story of conflict, wars between good and evil that will never end. Would you have only evil nations make war? Would you have only the Hitler's and Stalin's have armies? What if these God forsaken Islamic terrorists had the best weapons, instead of us? Would the world be a better place because of it? Are you so daft as to think that their hate would stop if our arms were laid down?

Let me answer in this way. When the good is defending the weak, when the right is fighting to resist the wrong, when the free are liberating the enslaved and those who have no defense are being defended, and when, in the wake of war, democracy rises from the ashes, then that is a "just" war.

Q: Will America survive another 200 years?

A: The idea of America is embedded in the basic rights of man. Those rights are God given. They began with God, and they will never die. If America falls, another will rise to replace her. It has always been so, and it will always be.

Q: Should we have a black or woman president?

A: Politics, like everything else, should be a meritocracy. Whoever runs the best race, makes his or her case in the free market for ideas, and wins the election should be the president. If that person is black or a woman, then he or she should be the president.

Q: What black men would have been a good president?

A: Only men? Condoleeza Rice would be a good president. So would Hillary Clinton, for that matter. Eleanor Roosevelt could have been president. Black men? Certainly Frederick Douglass. Perhaps Martin Luther King, although I cannot imagine him doing more good than he did in the role he filled. He was the last great abolitionist, you know. He finished what Lincoln started. Colin Powell would do nicely, and I like this young fellow from Tennessee. Harold Ford is his name. He barks the party line now, but I bet in the White House he would grow into his own man. That tends to happen.

The exchanges went on and on. Two hours per day for two and a half weeks. Oddly, they all bought into the game, but they asked mostly about modern things. This development pleased Erasmus most of all. He never wanted to be a museum piece, and it pleased him that they wanted to know what he thought about the world now.

They were the embodiment of youth seeking wisdom, and they sensed naturally that gruff as he was, he had some of it.

So for this magical time they absorbed every drop of him, and he was in heaven.

The student forum and our preparations for the trip to New England and New York kept us very busy. As was his pattern, Erasmus seemed to rally physical strength when faced with a specific purpose. Teaching his students and preparing for a trip home were both very important to him, so his health and vigor improved. But we were still very short of time, so I was surprised to find the old man still had time to write another essay, and send another student minion to slip it through the slot in my door.

Youth

Those of us who founded this nation, save for Franklin, Washington, and a few others, were quite young. There were not many old men freezing at Valley Forge, and fewer still stopping British lead on the banks of Brandywine Creek.

Socrates once said that the world would not survive another generation, as the up and coming one was so bad. But alas, here we all are.

I have had both the fortune and burden to have lived a very long time. And to this day, I would rather be around the young than any other group. They are free, they question, they think, and they express. They have little experience, and many ideas. So they say stupid things and do even worse. It is the nature of youth, and it is not a bad thing.

The young need guidance more than protection. They need attention, and they seek instruction. They yell less and listen more than we think.

It is incumbent on us to play the game with them. Take them seriously, but don't let them run amuck. Listen to what they are saying, but remember it is we who are the teachers. Be confident and instruct, but don't demean. Let them get knocked down, but help them up. Enjoy watching them enjoy being young, and you will be young too.

And for God's sake, love them. They are, you see, so easy to love.

Tacitus

Chapter Fourteen
"Hamiltons and Burrs"

It was late spring of 2005, and the lecture class was now over. As a result, Erasmus and I had time to spend reviewing the work we had done, and tending to additional essays. I pressed, as always, about historical matters, and he continued to emphasize current issues.

The two intellectual giants of the founding period were no doubt Hamilton and Jefferson. Erasmus truly loved the former, and had developed a grudging respect for the latter. So it was no surprise that he viewed our efforts as an expansion of Hamilton's Federalist Papers, and that he borrowed the Jeffersonian concept for his own "Bill of Corrections". Erasmus saw these ten amendments as corrective to the excesses of modern liberalism that he considered untrue to the Founders' intent. Jefferson, who tended to view liberal excess as a virtue, would not have approved.

After the successful lecture series, I arranged for Erasmus to meet periodically with a small group of honors law students in the ONU library. This meeting was another concession in a series the old fellow continually extracted from me in order to actually teach students that he had come to believe were his. Looking back know, I think he had come to intellectually distrust the professors and their teachings as being too rife with opinion and too shallow in content.

Being one of those professors, I pointed out to him that his teachings were at their core often solely his opinions, and we sparred often on this issue. But there was no doubt that my students benefited from his instruction, so I my resistance was a token one. During one such meeting he was expounding on the legal case conflicts that emerged between Hamilton and Burr in New York courts soon after the Revolution. Erasmus was in the actual practice of law during the "Confederation" period, in the same office with Hamilton. As always, he was praising the virtues of Hamilton and disparaging "that scoundrel Burr."

I felt him drifting once again toward an anti-Burr tirade not germane to our discussion, so I decided to redirect him with a question.

"In your writings, sir, you have proposed constitutional corrections that would allow restrictions on members of the Bar as concerns advertising. I know that you hold any advertisement that actually encourages parties to sue in particular contempt. But these proposals would also limit actions in civil law and cost lawyers vast sums of money. What are your thoughts about lawyers in our society today, and about the state of civil law?" I was going to stop here, and yield the floor to the ancient barrister so he could answer my question and reorient the discussion. He loved this particular topic, and had passionate views on it, so my bringing it up had him chomping at the bit.

But thankfully, from somewhere in that place in a person's mind where good ideas suddenly appear, a question shot into my brain and directly to my lips. It opened the gates to a flood of fascinating dialogue between the students and my old friend. The question was this; "Is the modern lawyer, in your opinion, Mr. Milton, a Hamilton, or is he a Burr?"

"You bait me to emotion, sir, and your attempt to guide me to an area about which you know I hold intense beliefs has not gone unnoticed," he replied with a chuckle. "But as I hold you in high regard as a gentlemen, and know the education of these young barristers is your goal, I will attempt to respond to your questions without becoming overly excited."

"Allow me to address the latter question first," he began. "My first thought is to expand your list of honorable lawyers from just Hamilton to include Adams, Marshall, Jefferson, Lincoln, and the like. It is also my personal experience that there are, in fact, in modern law many Hamiltons, and I have worked with a great number of them. However, it is my belief, sadly, that in law today we have not enough Hamiltons, and a growing number of Burrs."

He turned now to address the students. "You see, my young friends, modern law sees a lawyer only as an advocate, and trusts solely in the adversarial system and competition between attorneys to cause the truth to naturally ooze forth at trial. But this exclusive trust is folly.

A Hamiltonian lawyer knows he is also an officer of the court itself, a servant of the law, and a champion for equity when its balance has been disturbed. His obligation to his client is the best representation of his client's case before the law. But it does not extend to attempts to knowingly mislead, nor to distort or repress that which he knows to be true. His ultimate fidelity is to the law."

Like Pilate to Jesus, I asked, "What is law?"

Erasmus laughed again, tickled by the biblical reference.

"The rascal Burr once said that the law was anything that could be convincingly stated and effectively argued," replied the old King's College lawyer. "If Burr was on the side of truth, it was merely by coincidence. Law as he defines it is mercenary and has no respect for truth. Injustice becomes anything that inhibits the goals of the party paying his fee, and truth is to be squelched if its revelation defeats his cause. My Hamilton scoffed at this notion." He continued, "The law is truth, and the impartial application of its simple meaning without political or financial agenda is all that stands between us and the tyranny of courts who decide what the law should say, not what it does say."

Erasmus had taken the sudden leap from a lawyer respecting truth when it conflicts with client interest, and jumped to courts that substitute agenda for law. He saw both as the same issue, as a lack of fidelity to the law as simple truth.

The issue was more complicated, and he knew it. So I called him on the point of fact, and as always he rose to the challenge.

"Ah, so a strict structuralist is a good lawyer, and an expansionist jurist is not?" I baited.

"Not so," he parried. "An expansionist will modify free speech to keep up with the invention of the Internet, privacy rights to keep pace with surveillance technology, and civil rights to reflect our maturing understanding of equality. What he will not do is place in the law that which is not there. Nor will he, to earn a contingent fee, suppress, distort, or exclude the truth, nor make a case for what he knows to be a lie."

Erasmus was a master debater, and one of his favorite techniques was to refute your point then turn from you to another listener. As if his point was so obviously irrefutable as to have no reply, he would simply ignore your effort to respond and address someone else. Employing this technique now, he turned again to the students. "Today, my young friends, to my great disappointment, I see the Bar inhabited by too few Hamiltons, and a growing number of Burrs. To be greatly disturbed by the direction of our profession, one need only watch television. That 'lawyer' fellow who buys commercials in which he encourages neighbors to sue one another, using a cartoon where his head turns into a tiger!

In days where lawyers could self-police, that young man would have received a good cane whipping from real barristers as they dragged him kicking and screaming to the tar and feather pot."

"So what is the state of civil law, my friend?" I asked. "What case should be brought, what person defended, what interest argued? Are we unredeemable?"

"I hesitate, good man, to answer, for I know many a good man practicing today, and I impinge him not. But I dare say, I know of nothing that is doing more harm to the many, for the enrichment of the few, than the modern evolution of civil law."

"That's quite a statement, sir. How is it supportable?" I goaded the old man. I was familiar with his views on this subject, and they were radical. In asking the question I knew he would enter into a rant, and it was one that I wanted these young people to hear.

"My good man," he shot back. "Have you ever heard a single statement pass these lips that was not followed by a battalion of proofs rushing to its defense? Consider this example as my proof. When I was a young man, you could die from an infection of the kidneys emanating from a simple kidney stone. Now a person with completely diseased kidneys can live for years, waiting for a transplant, using mechanical dialysis.

"Yet just this week," he continued, "I saw a Texas law firm advertise that if anyone watching the commercial had recently been to a dialysis clinic, and had recently been hospitalized, then they may be entitled to a monetary settlement.

"Now it takes no genius to know that someone on dialysis is quite ill, and the chance of recent hospitalization is quite high. Now add to this mix an astute lawyer willing to vilify the first available deep pocket, regardless of who was harmed and who did the harming, and you see the commercial for what it is—a scoundrel trolling for potential members of a manufactured liability class so that he may enrich himself. He need only find an uninformed jury and an insured target. Then he can develop any legal position that 'can be convincingly stated and effectively argued.' Sound familiar?"

"And what of the truly injured? Who will care for them? " I challenged.

"And who always cared for them?" he quickly retorted, having, as usual, anticipated my question. "It was the local family lawyer, having empathy for his clients, caring for their condition, and knowing that to serve them well he must have a reputation with the court that he would further only claims he felt had true merit. He was a Lincoln, an Adams, and a Hamilton.

Now such good men practicing law are put out of business by interstate franchise lawyers selling class action suits and dog bite claims like peddlers selling snake oil and lame horses."

I responded, "So local lawyers, like small farmers, suffer from an economic sea change in an industry. Where, then, is the societal harm you claim?" I should have known better than to advance an economic argument. This old man was a compatriot of our own first national economist, and he was up to the task.

"When a lawyer knowingly disregards truth and advocates for injustice, and the system rewards him with a percentage cut of the spoils, however large, the economic results are foreseeable. You, as a man of letters, should know this," he chastised. "Take, for example, my earlier story of the Texas shyster. Ultimately, this man and his ilk will drive up the cost of insurance and the risk of loss for dialysis providers and device manufacturers alike. The capital applied to such ventures will face higher and higher risks as companies are vilified. Rates of return will fall, as will the numbers of providers of care. Patients will pay higher prices for lower supplies of less advanced care, and will go without treatment that foregone research would have provided from capital that has now sailed for safer ports of call. To put it most simply, some people will die because of the greed of a Texas lawyer."

He turned again to the class of young students. "This effect goes beyond medical devices. Areas of the country cannot get trauma care for head injuries, do not have adequate supply of obstetricians, and doctors flee to states that allow self-insurance and naked practicing in medicine. Goods are over priced, and the poor over pay for services.

"Good local lawyers disappear," he continued, "and true claims go unrepresented, while the people as a whole are taught that they are never responsible for the consequences of their own choices and behavior. The civil law is now a lottery, and the culprit is the greed of the Bar. Truth has not been barred from civil complaint; it just is not as relevant a factor. A civil lawyer all too often does not advise his client on whether or not his claim is actionable, but instead on its monetary worth. What do I think of tort law, you ask? And I tell you, it has totally lost its way. That is what I think of civil law."

This was one of those times where Erasmus had delivered an oral version of an essay, and it fell upon me to write it down later. He was a powerful speaker, and as I looked at the young students, they were sitting stunned in their chairs.

"You have been indicted," I told them. "Indicted for entering a profession whose honor needs redeeming. You will take many ethics classes over the years, but none so effective as today's. My old friend has addressed you for a reason. He is telling you to be a Lincoln, a Hamilton, an Adams, and not to be a Burr. Join those men of honor in your profession who would take it back from the lawyers whose heads turn into carton characters and who live to sue their neighbors. Do good work, do it well in the service of truth and the law, aid honorable people in just claims, and you will make a fine living doing so. In the end, as in all things, you must choose who you will serve."

It is indeed possible to argue that Erasmus overstated his case, I think, in the area of civil law. But there was a purpose in reaching the audience to whom he was speaking. I drove him home that night, and the next day when I arrived at my office at ONU, a student delivered an envelope from my friend. It contained another essay from our mutual philosopher, Tacitus.

Accountability

I was recently taking my mid-day meal at an establishment in a town not ten minutes from my home in Lafayette. My adopted home village, as you know, was named for my comrade and true friend of liberty, the dear Marquis. This other town also had an interesting name, named as it was for the capital of Peru.

It was called Lima, Ohio, mispronounced with a hard I, as it is the habit of Americans today to mispronounce nearly everything.

I was eating what in most periods of history would have been considered healthy food, a virtual banquet prepared in a clean environment free of food borne disease. But today it is much maligned under the general category of "fast food." It is a wonder, I think, that for an almost immeasurably low percentage of the modern American household income, one can purchase a frozen milk whipped with sugar and chocolate, potatoes deep fried wonderfully in the finest lard, and a ground steak cooked and placed between two pieces of bread. And most amazingly, no matter what the time of year, fresh vegetables— tomatoes, lettuce, and the like—can be placed between the buns or ordered in a salad.

I eat this food because I enjoy it. I am perfectly aware that if I eat it too much it will harm me. I am also aware that to buy it costs me, per meal, about twenty minutes of paid minimum labor, a historical wonderment compared to any other time in history. This fact is also true of virtually every other kind of food. In fact, it is a wonder as well that we live in a time where one of the major health problems in our society is that a subsistence level of calories, the goal of every government since cave dwellers first picked a chief, is so cheap and available that everyone in our country is getting fat.

In another strange commentary on our times, it has become necessary for our government, in order to protect our personal choices and liberty of lifestyle, to pass laws to not allow lawsuits against food providers when people choose to overeat or allow their children to do so.

Oddly, as I sat reading my Colby alumni magazine and enjoying my wonderful "frosty," my mind drifted to a conversation at the next table. Two young women were discussing all the things that young women discuss: their loves, their work, and their lives. As is the norm for us all, they also discussed money, and apparently one of them didn't seem to have quite enough of it. She recited to her friend the extent of her bills (they were many), and the extent of her income (not quite so much as her bills). In exasperation, she exclaimed to her friend, "I need to either inherit a fortune, win the lottery, or sue somebody."

There, my friend, is where the common man places the civil law. It rests beside the chance inheritance of a dead relative's wealth, and an abominable state numbers racket that targets the hope of the poor.

As social welfare payments that require no work are the great destroyer of self-reliance and social economic mobility, so too have lawsuits become the great destroyer of accountability. No longer are they limited to actions to enforce contracts or to set right the damage to one party which was caused by the provable negligence of another.

They are instead vehicles upon which social activists and advocates force social policy upon us, and where an industry of franchise lawyers mine the black pits of class actions for the contingent pot of gold.

In the process, we are never responsible from ourselves, never ascribed with the ability to choose for ourselves, and thus we are in need of protection from ourselves. We are never at fault, never accountable. But fear not, we infants have "advocates" to protect us.

Since these "advocate tyrants" that would protect us from ourselves have been only partially successful in outlawing personal lifestyle choices and accountability, they use the civil law to accomplish what government power cannot: de facto prohibition. And in the process, accountability is destroyed. If I am fat, the food company or hamburger merchant has made me so. If I am a drunkard, then not I but the purveyor of spirits is to blame. If I as a man have a sexual affair, I have been seduced. If I as a woman get drunk and succumb to the advances of a cad, I am raped. If I partake of tobacco, first identified as harmful by Sir Walter Raleigh in the court of Elizabeth the First, it is the evil tobacco company who tricked me into this vice. I am never at fault, never unwise, never negligent, never willing to take a future risk to obtain current enjoyment from a risky behavior, and I am never accountable. But you must also be warned, if I am not empowered to choose to harm myself, I am not free.

Civil law can be easily rendered again meaningful and just, and as such be a help, not a threat, to our freedoms. It must not be allowed to be hijacked by advocates and policy enforcement, but instead be limited to its proper intent. If you as an individual have been harmed by the negligence of another, then you may seek redress in the courts to put you in, as much as possible, the shoes you were in prior to the tort. To the extent you harmed yourself, you are entitled to no such redress.

Secondly, if you sign a contract, you must do what it says. If you do not, the other party may seek redress to require that it be enforced.

The law, you see, is not a game in which the best barrister wins. It is about the consistent application of rules to live by. It is about the protection of individuals and their ability to be left alone to live peaceably, not about telling them how to do so.

To redeem our legal system, we must restore the concept of accountability and disempower the advocate. We must end class action, and limit contingent fee. We must insist on real harm truly caused by the party being sued before liability is imposed, and we must accept that self-harm is a cost of personal liberty, and not empower our government to protect us from it. Without such change, the profession of Lincoln will not be redeemed.

Tacitus

Chapter Fifteen
The Battle of the Tennessee Waffle House
(The last battle of the Civil War)

It was now the summer of 2005, classes were out, and Erasmus and I were approaching the completion of our work. We were planning a trip to Atlanta, and Erasmus was excited to join us as he had on our trips to St. Augustine and New York. He was noticeably more frail, yet anxious to again revisit the South.

We began our trip early on a Saturday morning, and by early afternoon we were crossing the Kentucky-Tennessee state line. To placate my son Matthew, I promised we would stop to eat at a somewhat famous breakfast food chain called the Waffle House. It was way past breakfast time, which mattered little to Matthew, so we pulled off of I-75 to visit the Waffle House in Cleveland, Tennessee.

We strolled into this franchise chain, more of a lunch counter than a sit down restaurant, made famous by its "down home" friendly atmosphere, country food, and decidedly blue-collar class of patron. We were happy to be out of the car, and Erasmus was, as always, immensely enjoying a chatty conversation with Matt. Now Matthew, as you know, is our youngest, adopted at birth, and a bi-racial African-American. So walking into this Waffle House was an oddly dressed New Englander, my obviously Hispanic wife, my black son, and I. As always, we were a somewhat curious group.

As we sat enjoying hash browns covered with cheese, waffles, grits, bacon, and other country fare, I noticed a man who appeared to be about the age of Erasmus, who came out of the restroom and sat across from our booth at the lunch counter. He sported an old dirty ball cap with a confederate "stars and bars" sown on the front, a scruffy beard, and an old shop coat. He sat staring at us in a way that showed he didn't care if we noticed, and if looks could kill we would have all been dead. My family had names for such occasional stares ("social dinosaur looks" and "cracker glances" are my two favorites) and we had long ago given up being offended, so I paid the old fellow no mind.

Erasmus, on the other hand, drew up in a defensive posture, and returned fire with an equally hostile stare. I was taken aback when I saw my old friend's eyes, and in them I saw what I could only describe as rage. He suddenly looked away to Beda, asked in his old world way to be excused, took up his walking cane, and headed to the restroom.

Moments later, as Erasmus exited the restroom, I heard a scuffle behind me. Beda exclaimed, "Oh my God, Bob," and I turned around just in time to see three small pieces of paper fly into the face of the old boy with whom he had recently exchanged hate-filled visual volleys.

"Are these yours?" Erasmus hissed at the old man.

Rising from his seat, the old man screamed back, "They are, old man, and I'll put them back as soon as you and your mongrel family git outta here and git back on that highway, headin north, I reckin."

"South," Erasmus retorted. "Like I did once before with Sherman, you rebel bastard. And since I seemed to have had the misfortune of not putting a musket ball in your great grandfather's empty head, this will have to do."

Just as quickly as he had spoken, Erasmus raised his cane and brought it crashing across the old man's brow. Before the old rebel could respond, the walking cane eagle struck again, this time squarely in the old man's groin. Down he went, out of the fight. A younger man rose to the old reb's defense, but was met with another thrashing blow to the head, and the eagle tipped walking stick sent him crumbling to the floor.

Erasmus stooped down and put his knee on the younger man's chest, at the same time producing from his vest a wooden handled silver pistol that looked like something from an old Errol Flynn pirate movie. The cock of this old cap and ball pistol snapped loudly into the firing position, and the barrel rested against the young man's temple.

"You know old reb here?" Erasmus asked the younger man.

"Yes, sir," he replied.

"Then I'd get his secessionist ass to the hospital and have that gash on his head tended to. Tell the doctor he got his nose too close to an eagle, courtesy of Colonel Erasmus Milton, 12th Regiment, New York Mounted Volunteers."

The younger man then carried the defeated old confederate to his pickup truck, which thankfully had no shotgun in its back window. As they left, Erasmus returned to the table, apologized to Beda for the disturbance, kindly kissed Matthew on the head, and returned to his breakfast. I noticed in the background that the Waffle House manager was hanging up the phone.

When the sheriff arrived, I insinuated without outright lying that I was Erasmus' lawyer. As we were leaving I instructed Beda to get a room at the Holiday Inn across the street, and I would call her on my cell phone from the Cleveland, Tennessee, city jail. Moments before, Erasmus Milton, staff officer for

General George Washington, Under Secretary of the Treasury for Alexander Hamilton, hero of Saratoga, stormer of Yorktown redoubts, advisor to President Lincoln, wealthy industrialist, and Founding Father, had handed me his cane and proudly offered his wrists to the waiting handcuffs of the Cleveland, Tennessee, police.

As we left, I looked down and noticed, amidst the blood of the defeated confederate, three business card sized recruiting tracts. Each one had on it a small sketch of a hooded man, a web site address, and the words, "You are needed now by the Knights of the Ku Klux Klan."

After we had arrived at the jail and Erasmus was processed, he was put in a large common cell. It was still relatively early for a Saturday night, so it was nearly empty. The sole occupants were an old black man, a young white boy dressed all in black with gothic makeup and a fascinating number of nuts, bolts, and studs piercing various places on his face, and a local black minister. The minister had been sent there on a mission by the old black fellow's wife, to convince him to give up liquor and come home to Jesus or to "not come home at all."

I sat in the hallway, listening in amazement as Erasmus took no note at all that he had been jailed, and instead went from person to person engaging in an increasingly excited vocal exchange. He started first on the young boy, telling him it was all right to be a rebel in your youth. He concluded his speech with "Just make sure to find a cause worthy of your rebellion. Don't waste your righteous, unrealistic, idealistic youth on things as trivial as your clothes, your haircut, your music, or your curfew time. Make sure if you are ever in jail again, it is in the service of a "Glorious Cause". The boy, by this time enraptured by Erasmus' speech and in tears, rose and hugged the old man, and they laughed together.

Erasmus then turned excitedly to the black minister. "How goes the movement, man? Have we reached the mountaintop? Have the spawn of old Bedford Forrest been replaced with those who love liberty? Does freedom ring in the land of old Jim Crow?"

Before the minister could reply, Erasmus looked toward the old black man, who for a moment had hoped he would be saved by this strange white Yankee from further attempts to bring him to sobriety. "This old man should heed your words, preacher," Erasmus began again. "The bottle is a strong demon indeed, my beloved Elena always said. But old Martin Luther, the first one, brother, the German, he was right." Erasmus voice and tempo were rising now, catching the emotion of the moment and his little congregation was following. "A mighty fortress is our God, a bulwark never failing. 'A champion comes to fight,' he wrote in his hymns, my good man, 'with weapons of the spirit. You ask who this may be. The Lord of Hosts is he. And he will win the day!'"

"Amen," shouted the minister. "He will win the day!"

"Dr. Franklin was wrong, my friends. Life is not found in rules to live by. It is about faith and faith alone. By God, old fellow, no man can believe Jesus by his own intellect. The message, it's too incredible. But faith, my boy, faith will take you home!"

"Amen, my brother!" shouted the minister. Now jumping up and down, he called on powers God has reserved in our world exclusively for southern black ministers. "Jesus is the champion. Jesus will take away the drink, my brother" he sang to the old black man. "Jesus will take those spikes from your face, and replace them with redemption, the redemption of the cross, through the spikes driven into his hands, the spikes driven into his feet. Oooohhhhh Lord, show us the way!" he shouted rhythmically to the young white gothic.

"And knock down the mighty, and lift up the poor," chimed in the young white boy.

"And make all men equal," shouted Erasmus with delight.

"And stop the violence, oh Lord," sang the old black man in a deep baritone voice, "and end the anger, and the hatred, and please, oh Lord, stop the violence, and give us peace."

Stopping suddenly, Erasmus looked at his little jailhouse congregation. The others stopped as well, wondering what had suddenly driven the emotion from their old leader. Erasmus, as if stung by the old drunken man's prayer, quietly said, "Amen." He hugged the boy and the two black men, and sat down.

"Peace," the old man said quietly again, and the jailhouse revival settled quietly into a peaceful silence.

Out in the hallway, my observation of this amazing exchange was interrupted by the voice of a young deputy. "Does the old Yankee belong to you?" he asked.

"Yes," I replied rather sheepishly.

"Well, the judge stopped in across the street for some coffee and a piece of pie, and he heard the whole story. He wants to see you both in his chambers, now," the deputy ordered.

The deputy unlocked the cell and went in to face Erasmus. He had to wait as my old friend went to each occupant, saying touching good-byes. He charged the old man to conquer the bottle as if it were an enemy on the field. He thanked the pastor, and told the young boy that the best way to change the world was to educate himself, acquire economic power, and use it for the good of his community.

Erasmus met me in the hall with a broad smile. "I sure reminded old reb who won the war, didn't I?" he bragged like a schoolboy.

"Hush up," I said. "Don't make things worse than they already are. You broke about a dozen laws, we are going before a local judge, and you could have killed that stupid old man."

"Old Henry Cobb?" chuckled the deputy. "You couldn't kill him with a sack of hand grenades. He's already home from the emergency room, after seventeen stitches. Serves the old bastard right. I told him a dozen times to stop leaving those stupid cards all over town or someone's gonna kick his old cracker ass." He then knocked on an office door, stuck his head inside, and then looked back at us. "This way. The judge will see you now."

We walked into the judge's private chambers and, as soon as we did, I actually had to suppress a smile.

Sitting behind a huge mahogany desk, in a black robe, was a huge, stern-looking judge. His name was the Honorable William Douglass Carver, and he was very, very black.

"Are you this man's lawyer?" thundered Judge Carver. Thankfully Erasmus saved me from a lie, and stated, "I am an attorney, sir, a long-standing member of the New York Bar. While I have no license from the great state of Tennessee, I am a graduate of King's College, and am qualified to represent myself."

"So you are, sir. So no doubt you understand I could charge you with felony assault should I desire to do so?"

"I do, Your Honor," replied Erasmus, "and if your duty so dictates, you should do so, but first let..."

The judge cut off Erasmus at this point. "You, sir, will say nothing. You have come to my town and disturbed it, and interrupted my Saturday evening to boot. You have broken the law, sir, and now I must decide what to do with you. Now I know old Mr. Cobb, and I also heard what provoked you. Cobb is a black-hearted bigot, and I have wanted to thrash him many times myself. Now I ask you, Colonel. [His addressing Erasmus as Colonel took us aback, and made us understand just how complete a report the judge must have gotten about the events at the Waffle House.] Would you deny this old man his rights? He says and does things with which you disagree. But he, unlike you, makes no mischief nor breaks no laws in my city. Unless being an idiot has been made illegal, I do not know of any crimes he has committed. I am committed to the law, sir, and if he acts on his idiocy I will deal with him. But you, sir, tell me. Do you believe in freedom only for people with whom you agree? Do you believe in the law only when you feel like obeying it?"

Erasmus fell silent, chastised in the same fashion as he had been by the old black man seeking peace and an end to violence. "You are right, sir," he replied to the judge. "And for the second time this evening I have been made to look upon my pride and imperfection. For my actions and the mayhem I have visited upon your community, I am truly sorry."

"You are also convicted, Colonel, of disorderly conduct. You are fined $600 plus costs, which you shall remit to the bailiff. And you are charged to make no such mischief in my city again."

"Yes, sir," Erasmus replied.

"I have one more question for you," Judge Carter said. "The 12th Regiment of New York Mounted Volunteers, I understand you mentioned this unit during your misbehavior earlier this evening."

"Yes, I did, sir. And you know of them?" Erasmus replied.

"Know of them? They were a civil war unit of free New York black men. They were funded, equipped, and commanded by a group of rich, white, Hudson River valley abolitionists. They were the only cavalry unit in the entire United States Colored Troops, and riding among them was my great grandfather, Master Sergeant George Carver. I don't know how you knew of them, sir, but that knowledge saved you a month in my jail.

"By the way," he continued, "that pistol is quite a piece, and if I had any sense at all I would confiscate it and keep it in my collection as trustee for the City of Cleveland. But I trust you will never draw it again in my jurisdiction, so my deputy will return it to you when you pay your fine at the front desk. You are free to go."

Erasmus then nodded his head, and we turned to leave the office. At the door, Erasmus turned back to the judge. "Your Honor, you know, your great grandfather, Sergeant Carver, he was a good soldier and a good man."

Erasmus paid the fine from his old but well stocked money pouch, collected his pistol and we went to the Holiday Inn.

When we entered the room, we found Beda holding a weeping Matthew, who was convinced that Papa Milton was going to jail, never to return. My glance told Erasmus that I was none too pleased with this additional consequence to the events of the evening, and he quickly took to comforting the boy.

The next morning we went on to Atlanta, visited historical sites and modern wonders of all kinds, and returned home a week later. On our first night back, Erasmus was quite tired and not feeling at all well, so Beda insisted he stay with us. At some point in the night, perhaps unsettled from not being in his own home, or perhaps his dreams of past times again intruded on his rest, Erasmus rose and wrote again. The next morning, on the old table beside my books in the "smart room", I found an envelope from our friend Tacitus.

Redemption

There is no perfect man, save one. My dear old friend Dr. Franklin once told me that the teachings of Jesus the Christ were the greatest system of rules to govern men's lives as had ever or ever would be devised. Yet those of us who would champion the liberty and justice demanded by those teachings often find that it is ourselves who fall most short in the living of them.

I have, in my life, gone to war many times in the service of the "Glorious Cause". Each time I took life, and many times I nearly lost my own. As the end nears for me, I tremble at the knowledge that I will soon know if I was right or wrong in doing so. I cannot say for sure, although my heart was true in each endeavor.

I recently returned from the sight of one such struggle, where I had once gone to war. My comrades and I first went there as abolitionists bound for glory, to free the oppressed and bring the year of jubilee to those who were in bondage. By struggle's end, we had seen such killing, such carnage, and while we ended slavery and saved the Union, we won not the hearts of the ones we had conquered.

I have ridden again, with my new family, the route I once rode with Sherman—this time not to burn and kill, but only to ride. I saw, while on this ride, signs that perhaps the unsurrendered heart has finally begun to yield.

The bigotry that made slavery possible still exists, but it is unaccepted. Freedom, while not universal, is universally acknowledged as right. Prejudice, still in many hearts, is seen as a flaw even in one's self.

No person is perfect, no region is pure or blameless, and no country is without its flaws. But those of my brethren who served the "Cause" on so many fields would, I think, be proud of us. We have cleansed our land of slavery, cleansed our laws of injustice, and we are on our way to cleansing our souls of the remnants of bigotry.

We have far to go, my blessed land, but we have left the land of Egypt and we are now trudging together toward Jordan. We have been in the wilderness of bigotry and hate for many years. And perhaps like the Hebrews of old, it is our children, not us, who God will let see the Promised Land. But I see signs that we are closer, signs that we are nearing the goal. I now believe that we will reach the mountain top, and from it our beloved land itself will someday sing, "Amazing grace, how sweet the sound, that saved a wretch like me."

Tacitus

Chapter Sixteen
Letter to a Young Gentleman

How does one deal with the eccentricities of a walking, breathing, piece of history? What does a gentleman who is committed to the cause of abolition, a cause he views as so just and pure as to be divinely ordained, do when he is confronted with a bigoted scallywag on the streets of New York in 1785? My guess is he may give the scoundrel a sound cane whipping and be congratulated by his friends for the fine effort.

How do I explain to that same gentleman that in 2005, that the same reaction may rightly land him in a Tennessee jail?

My dear, beloved old friend had done a much better job than I could have ever done in keeping up with the times over two and a half centuries. But the task, alas, was imperfectly completed.

I had to tell Erasmus upon our return that it was unacceptable that he should rise to violence and put the safety of my family at risk in such a setting as a Tennessee Waffle House. I had to tell him that I was particularly upset that he had done so in front of my son, who, at eleven years old, worshiped the old man like a grandfather. "What sort of example does that set?" I asked.

Erasmus stoically endured the lecture, and his sadness was palpable. I was soon saddened as well, for over the next two weeks I did not hear from him. Nor did he make any of his now famous appearances at the law school in Ada. Students approached me, inquiring about his health, and I promised to check in on him. But I knew it was my stinging rebuke that kept him away.

After two weeks, another student courier slid an envelope through the mail slot. I was much relieved, and naturally thought Erasmus had again written a "Tacitus" essay. Such was not the case. Instead, the envelope was addressed as follows:

"Master Matthew Robert Sielschott, Esq. In care of his father, my dear friend Robert Sielschott"

Inside was a written letter to my young son, one that he will no doubt cherish forever. It was as close to an apology as Erasmus could probably write and in its crudely charming way it was quite marvelous. It read as follows:

"Dear Master Matthew,

Nothing would please me more, my dear boy, than to see you grow into a gentleman of substance, one who conducts his affairs with honor and integrity, who cares for his wife and children, who works hard at his labors, and who showers love on his family and charity on his community.

These are the things, young Matthew, that define a gentleman. Not old ideas of swords, dueling, pistols, and chivalry.

A man's honor is woven into the fabric of his life. It is inside him, not outside. And if he himself must constantly declare it, then he should consider whether or not he has made it sufficiently apparent by the way he lives.

Recently you observed me make a grievous error, one that I fear in later life might cause you to act rashly or erroneously should you emulate my conduct. I sought wrongly, through unprovoked violence, to defend you and your lovely mother. In fact, the insipid serpent that I so roundly thrashed at that waffle establishment had not, in any way, indicated that he intended violence toward you. And while it is true that he was a black-hearted bigot of the worst sort, most deserving of a good thrashing, it was in fact my pride and my desire to display courage in front of you and your mother that caused me to overreact toward that poor, unfortunate bastard.

For this, young Master Matthew, I sincerely apologize. I was wrong to strike the man, wrong to draw my pistol, and wrong to have you witness my being handcuffed by the young constable. I mistook pride and self-righteousness for honor and in doing so set a horrible example for a young man that I love beyond all reckoning.

I have now, for the second time in my life, in the person of your father, a friend who is as close to me as a brother could be. The last time I had such a friend, I lost him to a duelist's bullet.

My dear friend Alexander, you see, was shot and killed fighting a duel over a minor affront to his honor. It was an insult given by a man not worth the spilling of a single drop of blood, and the affront was known by all as being unworthy of even a response. Yet due to his sense of honor—no, his sense of pride—my beloved Alexander could not let it go. So he went off to duel, and was lost to us all.

So pick your battles, young man. I would lay down my life for you and your parents should any danger threaten them, and to do so would be an act of great honor. I myself was wounded, and many of my close friends fell, in the service of our "Glorious Revolution".

But never draw your sword, my young friend, in the service of your own pride or reputation. Your pride is not worth the spilling of the most wretched scoundrel's blood, and if your reputation needs protected, then look instead to your public life and the knowledge of your neighbors that you are an honorable man. This is your honor's best defense. It is a lesson I should have learned when I lost my dear Hamilton, yet the thought of you seeing me cane that wretched old man has caused me to learn it again.

I ask your forgiveness, Master Matthew, and that of your father. He is a good man, and looks only to your care and rearing to honorable adulthood. I envy him as he recipient of the love and devotion of his family, and you should honor and obey him always. I have missed you so, but without his blessing and confidence I must for now keep my own company. I look forward to the receipt of your pardon, so that I may again warm my soul in the company of my little friend and his wonderful family.

With sincere regards, I remain your willing servant and loyal friend,

Erasmus Milton"

I stood in the doorway, tears running down my face. I was again touched and amazed by the dignity, grace, and affection displayed by the old man. He had stayed away, thinking I was angry, and thinking I felt he was a bad influence on my son. It was apparent too, the extent to which he had fallen in love with my family, and particularly with my little boy. Having been for so long denied the role of the adoring grandfather, unnaturally lost to his odd affliction, he was now relishing it. And I had, unknowingly, made him feel that that role was now at risk. I felt horrible that he had taken my rebuke in this way, and I knew I must set matters right again between my son and my old friend.

I called Matthew into the smart room, where he had so often listened to the old man's stories. There I read him the letter. I explained that the old codger in the Waffle House was an angry, old, and prejudiced man, who hated people like he and his mother because they were brown instead of white. I told Matthew that this old man belonged to a group who hurt people for that reason, and that this had made Erasmus very angry, especially because Papa Milton loved him and his mother so much. I then explained that Erasmus was still wrong to have hit the man, and that this letter meant he was very sorry.

"We need to go see him, Dad, and tell him its okay," Matthew said.

"Yes we do, son. Go get your jacket," I replied.

We drove the short ride down Route 81 to the village of Lafayette, past the veteran's monument, and up the lane to the only house in the little village that could rightly be called a mansion. A form waited in the window, watching us as we approached. As my son scrambled up the porch steps, the door flew open and Erasmus emerged.

"Master Matthew, my dear boy, I have missed you so," he exclaimed as he hugged his young companion. "You are just in time. The old widow Wilhelm has again left me cookies, and I am in need of help in tasting them. Oddly attractive, the old frau, especially for a German woman," he said to me with a wink.

"Would you like some milk as well? I bet you would like to see my old uniforms again. I'll fetch them while you eat your cookies."

On and on the old man went. I spent the afternoon eating the widow Wilhelm's cookies, sipping port of some unknown age and origin, and watching these two happy souls play away the day.

I never published Erasmus' letter to my son until the publication of this book. But I thought if you were to know him and to love him as I did, it was a letter you must see. I trust he will forgive the breach of confidence.

Chapter Seventeen
"Welcome Home, Mister Milton"

As you recall, my relationship with my old friend began with a bargain. I was to have his federalist essays published. He, in turn, was to allow me various interviews and access to his history. By the fall of 2005, Erasmus had fully kept his part of the bargain. He had given me full access to him, his papers, and his artifacts, and I had learned so much from him that I would never be the same.

I had during the course of our relationship made a second commitment, and it was now time to keep it. Erasmus wanted to go home one more time, and I had promised to take him. So I took a leave of absence from Ohio Northern for the month of October, ironically using a technique often employed by Erasmus. I told my department head that I must go on a "special mission of great importance" that involved astounding research that I could not divulge. Beda teased the old man about how he had corrupted my sense of honor with all these talks of secret missions. "Secrecy in the service of goodness, especially one that old ONU will soon realize, is not a betrayal of honor, my dear", he chuckled. "But you, like Elena, are a true compass for an ethical course, and I thank you." Beda laughed and blushed as the old man kissed her hand. Then she curtsied in response, a reaction to his chivalry that she knew he enjoyed.

Matthew and I packed the SUV for the long trip back to New York and New England. I said nothing to Matt, but in my heart I knew the purpose of our trip was the retracing of the old man's life for a final time. On October first we loaded Erasmus and Matt comfortably into the middle row of bucket seats, Beda and I got into the front, and I drove out of my driveway. We turned onto Slabtown road, then onto Interstate 75, and headed north.

At Bowling Green we turned northeast on Route 6, and passed through Fremont, Ohio, the town that claims itself as the home of President Garfield. Erasmus of course enlightened us that he was actually born in the village of Orange, east of Fremont, and oddly that he had attended college at Williams, a Massachusetts rival of his own Colby College.

Our first night was spent in the luxury suite of the old Breakers Hotel, now part of the Cedar Point amusement park in Sandusky, Ohio. The stately old lady overlooks Lake Erie, and was once the summer destination of choice for wealthy New York families seeking to escape the summer heat of the city. Such families would take a river steamer to Albany, a canal launch to Buffalo, and catch a Lake Erie packet ship to Sandusky Bay. Every boat along the way, we came to learn, was part of the East Coast shipping company owned by industrialist Erasmus Milton, and every dollar of ticket revenue added to his wealth.

During our brief one day stay, Erasmus regaled us with incredible stories of holding court in these stately dining rooms and parlors. There he traded barbs, insults, laughter, and at times whole fortunes with the likes of Henry Flagler, Thomas Edison, Henry Ford, and Diamond Jim Fisk.

"It was a time," he said, "when we convinced ourselves that wealth mattered above all, and that if a man's work made him a fortune, it made him also a better man than the one whose work merely earned him his daily bread.

"I am proud of my accomplishments, and I have used my fortune, I think, for the greater good," Erasmus noted. "But in this belief we had then, that we were in some way more worthy of blessing because of the blessing itself, I know now we were wrong."

We left Sandusky the next day, traveling west on I-90. We passed an old iron ore port at Ashtabula, once owned by one of Erasmus' enterprise companies. As industrial companies became more specialized, he spotted the trend and sold the ore shipping concern at the top of the market to the Steinbrenner family. That company founder's son, a Clevelander named George, eventually got out of the Erie ore shipping trade and bought a baseball team.

We stopped for our second night at Erie, PA. At the port there, restored as a floating museum, was a beautiful example of a pre-steam Erie sailing vessel.

The next day Erasmus insisted that we drive down to the dock at the historic park there, and tour the small, twin mast lake schooner.

As we strolled along the deck, Erasmus obnoxiously and continually corrected the guide, and eventually took over the tour himself. We all listened in amazement as he explained the history, workings, and operation of the wind driven sailing vessel.

"Many a trip I made on my own such vessels to Detroit, Toledo, past Mackinaw, through the straights, and the like. Stout little ladies they were, capable of running ahead of the nasty Erie storms that sneak up on a man making the shallow lake passage."

The next day we stopped at Buffalo and visited the site of the source of Erasmus' second huge fortune. It was here that he correctly predicted the economic impact of the Hudson and Erie Canal, and invested his profits from his revolutionary bonds into real estate and shipping at the lake end of the canal. His early trading posts and lake sailing sloops allowed him to establish dominance in trade at the Erie end of the manmade passage that would make him, once again, a very wealthy man.

After a day of history reliving Erasmus' life as an Erie shipping magnate, we left again on I-90. At Buffalo, this highway becomes the "New York Thru Way" and turns east toward New York and Boston.

As if affirming the brilliance of Milton, Clinton, and the other early supporters of the project, the highway follows the path, through Upstate New York, of the old Hudson and Erie Canal.

By the evening of our fourth day, we pulled into Albany, New York. Anxious about being able to get a room and concerned about the old man's comfort, I inquired about which motel he would prefer close to the highway. Erasmus muffled a chuckle, and directed me downtown.

We stopped in front of an older yet immaculate office building, where a valet came to greet us.

"Welcome back, Mr. Milton," he said. "Four years, has it been, sir? It is good to see you."

"And you, Charles. I've missed the old place. All is ready?" asked Erasmus in his reply.

"Oh yes, sir, as if you never left. Mr. Wendell is waiting to show you up, as well as your guests. I'll have Mr. Gregory see to the bags."

"Thank you so much, Charles. You are as efficient as ever," Erasmus replied with the punctuation of a substantial tip that would not have been affordable for a college professor from western Ohio.

Now Charles was an older black gentleman, about whom I to this day hold an extreme curiosity. He could best be described as an "old world" servant butler. His demeanor was one of public subservience, yet Erasmus always treated him with great respect and when interacting with the rest of the staff, he was totally in charge. He had obviously stayed in close touch with Erasmus, a secret about which I never had a clue. I got the impression that he had taken the old man's well being onto himself as his life's mission, and that he had been doing it for a long time. I got the immediate impression from his manner that he might be aware as we were of Erasmus' aging disorder, and I even wondered at times if he perhaps had a similar condition.

Charles escorted our group to the top floor of this grand building, where we were led by a servant into a magnificent suite of rooms: one for Beda and I, a spare room off of ours that Charles indicated with a smile had been "especially reserved for Master Matthew", and the master suite for the old man. Following Erasmus' earlier example, I was about to tip the servant when I heard Charles clear his throat and cast a glance of disapproval toward the servant's outstretched hand. "That will not be necessary, sir" Charles said to me. "Mister Milton had instructed that you are not guests, but are family, and are to be treated as long absent loved ones again returning home." He glanced at Beda, bowed, and exited.

I had noticed on the way to our rooms that at every turn along the way, we were greeted with, "Good to see you back, sir," "Welcome back, Mr. Milton," "I hear the project is going well, Mr. Milton," "I'm glad to hear the firm is well, Mr. Milton." For the life of me, I could not tell where the respect ended and the affection began, but whoever these people were, they loved this old man. Great deference was shown to me, and "Master Matthew" was given the absolute run of the building. But an odd reverence, bordering on awe, was directed toward Beda.

For the next several days we stayed in Albany. In our life back home, watching Erasmus interact at the college and in his little village, we never would have imagined him in this, his real world. During our time in Albany, Beda and I learned just how large and far reaching the life, fortune, and influence of our kindly old friend really was. He was, in every way save the physical, what was once called a "Titan".

We spent our time in Albany touring, via the hospitality of Erasmus' transportation staff, the various and sundry historical sights of the old capital. Erasmus was in his element, meeting with his firm's lawyers and boards, and then spending the evening with us, recounting the day's events. After reviewing our sight seeing events of the day, and playing with Matt, he would then retire with me to discuss the events of his own day. He voiced great frustration with the level of government involvement in his private enterprise.

I came to realize that while he may have regretted the decadence of the Gilded Age, he did miss the days when a man of business could conduct his affairs without the approval of dozens of agencies and regulators. "I cannot take a piss without a permit" he growled one evening as we discussed his business.

Early in this trip I had thought we were approaching the completion of our work on Erasmus' papers and essays, but his work in Albany indicated this was not the case. Working again in his offices had reinvigorated both his health and his combativeness. Hence he had the ever present Charles deliver to me one morning in my room an essay that was more true to his old self.

Law as Tyranny, Regulator as Tyrant

∽◌∾

I once heard a story from a talented and insightful writer and lawyer named Philip Howard, one he reproduced in his wonderful book *The Death of Common Sense*. Briefly, the story goes that a group of nuns of the Order of Mother Teresa had raised money to create a shelter for homeless men. New York loved the idea, and was selling them an old, run down, vacant building for a dollar. All was well. Sixty-five homeless men were going to have shelter, and an eyesore of a building was going to be put back to use. The world was going to be a better place. That is, until an idiot of a code inspector stopped the project because, he noted, all buildings over two stories must have an elevator and covered indoor fire stairs.

The law was the law, no exception could be made, and the sixty-five men stayed freezing in the streets, beaten by muggers, and starving for food.

The law, like the Sabbath, is made for man, not man for the law. My beloved Hamilton was right when he said that the law is to be worshipped, as it is our protector. But he, like all the Founders, studied and believed in the "common law". Not even the utopian Jefferson ever felt that government should be empowered to regulate our societal behavior in an exact way. Exact regulation without reasonableness is tyranny. The government should not be so powerful as to be able to regulate away every possible bad thing, nor should it be so foolhardy as to try. We elect people to serve our government because we think they have wisdom and sound judgment. They in turn appoint public servants for the same reason. Let us all resolve to tolerate the occasional bad apple, and allow our public servants to exercise some prudent, reasonable judgment.

I would propose today a law that simply reads as follows:

"All bureaucrats and regulators are hereby empowered to make exception to any regulatory requirement when, in their reasonable judgment, the enforcement of the regulation in a specific circumstance either works against the stated goal of the regulatory policy, or by the simple application of common sense it is evident that the public good suffers greater harm than the good produced by enforcement in this specific circumstance.

All such exceptions made are subject to administrative review and, if necessary, due process limited to one judicial hearing. Each exception is to be made due to a specific set of facts and circumstances, and is not to be construed as precedent."

"A loophole for abuse! A plan ripe for fraud!" the apostles of governmental goodness would cry. Fraud and abuse, of course, would at times happen. But, my dear country, you are regulating yourselves out of existence. Regulators who apply no judgment are petty tyrants, and regulation that tries to be so overwhelmingly inclusive as to cover every possible situation is tyranny.

Regulation is already here that tells people of commerce everything they can and cannot do. For individuals, such a world is not far behind. Soon all things harmful will be regulated: what we eat, drink, do, and don't do. Then regulations will come telling us what we can say, and finally what we can think. All in the name of goodness, and all enforced by unelected bureaucrats whose only reply to our petitions and complaints will be, "I'm sorry, but it is the law." Well I am sorry, my friend, but regulation does not, and should not rise to the level of law. Law grants rights to individuals, and restricts the power of government. Regulation, while at times necessary, takes away the rights of individuals, and empowers government to control us.

I am no Jeffersonian, as you know. But give the devil his due. I would paraphrase my old Virginia Jacobin as follows:

"If we can keep our government from regulating away all our commerce, our choices, and the control of our personal lives, all in the name of protecting us, then we will be happy."

Tacitus

Chapter Eighteen
The "Elena"

Having presumably put all his business affairs in order, Erasmus, at dinner that night, announced that the next day we would board his river launch and travel down the Hudson to his home.

The next morning we were greeted by an early summons from Charles, and our bags were taken to a waiting van. Erasmus was already in the company car, a sleek black Lincoln with a driver and an extra middle seat facing the rear. We were driven to the Albany marina, and there we boarded the Milton family launch. Never have I seen so much polished brass and mahogany. The antique vessel must have been eighty years old, but it was polished like a new craft, and its inboard diesel purred like a kitten. Across the stern, elegantly scripted in gold, was the name "Elena."

The crew consisted of a porter, a deckhand, and the captain, a Mr. J.P. Jones. As passengers we were joined by Charles, who while he did not function as part of the crew was intimately familiar with the craft and was treated with great deference. After we began our journey down the Hudson, the porter told us that the captain's real name was Patrick Cleveland, a former tug boat skipper from New York. I commented to Charles on the oddity of having a fictitious name for the captain of the craft. "Not as odd as one might think, Master Robert" he replied.

"Mr. Milton has had many friends and comrades in his life, and those who he finds honorable, he takes pleasure in likewise honoring. Hence the name of this craft. So 'in honor of an old friend,' as Mr. Milton had ordered, all skippers of the Elena shall be referred to on board as Captain J.P. Jones." From his demeanor I noticed that Charles was quite aware that the skipper was named after the legendary Revolutionary War hero and founder of America's first navy, John Paul Jones. Charles, I thought at the time, knew more about my old friend than he let on.

The cruise down the Hudson was gorgeous. We passed homes once occupied by the Vanderbilts, the Roosevelts, the Rockefellers, and the Morgans. We glided by the ancestral homes of every family of the Gilded Age. "Just a bunch of Hudson River dandies," chuckled Erasmus, as we gawked at the beautiful homes.

I commented to my host about the level of splendor and opulence, as is no longer seen in modern America.

"Such a level of splendor is no longer possible in an era where nearly half of any successful man's annual income is deemed to be immoral and is taken by the government," Erasmus lectured. "I kept 160 men working nearly five years building my home, and so did every other man on this part of the river. When we were done, we kept thirty of them on as staff.

Today such grandeur is seen as decadent, yet when legalized plunder is taken from us and squandered away by bureaucrats and vote buying politicians, it is seen as virtuous. God damn the income tax."

Just as the dear old fellow had ended his tirade, his face brightened and he pointed toward the shore. There, on a bluff above the bend in the river, was a huge complex of buildings, barns, and stables, with a lane leading up to a mansion as elegant as any we had thus far seen. "Casa de la familia," whispered Erasmus, "the home of my family."

Not surprisingly, we were met by staff, which swarmed the launch. Charles barked orders and everything was unloaded with military precision. He took great care in aiding Beda as she disembarked. She was treated with nearly as much affection and deference as the old man, and I definitely got the feeling of being a "third wheel" from the moment we set foot on the Milton Estate. Oddly, we were driven from the dock and up the lane to the mansion in a beautiful old horse drawn open carriage, and as we reached the front door the staff had aligned to greet us.

The staff's attitude toward Erasmus was the same as the staff in Albany. They had obviously also been made aware of who we were and our relationship to the old man. The chief butler, in charge of the household staff, reported to Charles that all was in readiness, then scurried the staff off to their duties.

He then turned to me with a bow. "I am honored to meet you, sir. Charles informs me that you are the gentleman who will rectify the historical injustice done the House of Milton. I am so pleased, as it has always troubled my master so." He then turned to Beda. "Madame, I welcome you to the Milton estates. You are everything Mr. Milton said you would be. It has been too long since such grace has reigned here." Charles then dismissed the chief butler, and turning finally to Erasmus, he said, "Sir, the study is prepared as you requested. If you will follow me."

We were then led into the study, which was without question the most complete and ornate personal library I have ever seen. "It is hardly the smart room, dear boy," Erasmus winked, "but for the next few days it will have to do. We have much work to complete."

As Beda entered behind us, I heard her gasp. Being preoccupied with the books, tables, and shelves full of amazing military and historic artifacts, I had failed to notice what she was now staring at. High above the huge stone fireplace, commanding the room with a shy smile, was a portrait. It was a picture of a dark-skinned, beautiful lady, dressed in period dress of the early 1800s. She gazed down at us with big brown eyes, and her resemblance to my own Beda was at the same time both eerie and astonishing. "Ah," said Erasmus, "I see you have met my lovely Elena."

Beda spent a week in paradise, wandering through the mansion, around the grounds, and taking trips on the launch. Matthew was given reign of the pool, and the indoor bowling alley. As Erasmus found it bordering on scandalous that I had not done so, he also gave strict instructions that Matthew was to be given daily riding lessons.

Erasmus and I, however, spent most of our days in the study. Under the watchful gaze of his Spanish beauty, we refined and expanded on his prolific "Federalist Papers." He further expanded on his interview questions from our time at ONU, and revisited his Bill of Corrections. We also reviewed, in great detail, which departments at Columbia and Colby were to receive the papers he had labeled and cataloged in the storage room off the study. His personal correspondence, he said, had been dealt with back in Lafayette, and I would understand that soon enough.

Each evening we would then walk the grounds and enjoy an elegant dinner. Erasmus, looking tired, would then retire.

During one such evening, after he had gone to bed, I sat in his study. Beda sat beside me as I smoked one of his exquisite old pipes and stared at the fire.

"Surely you've noticed," Beda said as she stared again at the lovely portrait.

"How could I not, honey?" I said. "She could be your sister, or your mother. Hell, look at her, she could be...you."

"It's kind of wierd, isn't it?" Beda replied.

"That he fell in love with a beautiful Spanish girl, and then met another one who looked just like her, 240 years later? What's weird about that?" I laughed.

Beda went on. "You remember my mom telling stories about old Mexico, coming here when she was young, and the old grandfather who claimed to be descended from the Spanish court. His last name was Garza, you know. You don't suppose... no, that would be just too strange."

"Honey," I replied. "For over a year I have been editing and publishing essays for a man who claims to be a contemporary of General Washington. He says he was Alexander Hamilton's best friend, and is the only living soul in America who despises Thomas Jefferson. He knows things, and possesses things, and has experienced things that only a person who was actually at the pivotal events of our country's history could have. He graduated from Columbia when it was still King's College, and they changed their name in 1778! This man held Hamilton's hand as he died, for God's sake. No, I think you are wrong. I don't think that for the rest of my life I will ever again use the words 'too' and 'strange' side by side in a sentence."

We laughed again, bid our good evenings to the lady of the house still staring down on us from above the mantle, and rose to go to bed. As I did, I noticed on the old writing desk an essay from our friend Tacitus. At Beda's request, I read it aloud.

Rest

Because of my odd affliction as concerns aging, I have had to travel farther than most men. I have been able to do more things, yet I have had to suffer more things as well. You see, most men see the sunrise and they know that after a day's work they will again lie down in their bed. As years pass, they know that after paying their tribute to their life's work, they will retire. And even the young know that some day they will age and die. The wise, in their aging, find faith, and they move without fear toward death.

Many a secular agnostic has ridiculed the faithful for their fear of death. If they were indeed true to their faith, would they not rejoice in the approach of their own demise?

But this is not fair. My old friend Dr. Franklin, as he aged and I remained in my youth, marveled at my health as compared to his own declining physical state. Discussing his imminent death, he once told me, "Dear boy, do not judge me in my fear, as it is not the destination we all dread, but the passage."

I have lived so long that this fear of the passage has faded away. I have tried to create a home for myself many times on this earth, only to have those who made it so age, die, and leave me again alone. I have learned in this time that God was wise in how he made our lives. In the morning we move toward the rest of the night. At the beginning of the week we move toward the rest of the Sabbath. At the peak of our careers we move toward the rest of our retirement. And in the end of our lives we move through death, toward our resting place with God. So all of creation, it would seem, moves toward rest.

I am tired. I long to lay down again with my Elena and close my eyes. I thank God that it will now not be so long. I am again a natural creature, and I am moving again toward rest.

Tacitus

Beda wiped a tear from her eye, and hugged me. "When I first saw him start to age, and figured out it was your publishing his essays, I wanted you to stop."

"I know," I said. "I've thought that same things many times."

"But look at her," she said, pointing at the portrait. "He must miss her so. You are doing a good thing, Robert."

"I hope so, but I will miss him. Matt will miss him."

"We all will, dear." She grabbed my hand, and we glanced again at the portrait of Elena, looking almost anxious now, and kinder. Hand in hand, we climbed the long staircase, where together we would rest.

Chapter Nineteen
Lady With A Torch

Erasmus took to his sick bed for a week, saying he needed to rest before the next leg of our journey. Beda nursed him, and the staff deferred to her every command. The incredible resemblance to the woman in the portrait was not lost on them, and it seemed to all, especially Erasmus, that the beautiful Elena Garza Milton was once again in command of her stately Hudson River manor.

After a few days, Erasmus emerged, looking frail but refreshed. The servant staff assisted him back to the launch, as the crew loaded all our belongings. You would think that they would be shocked at the seemingly sudden demise of their beloved master, yet they never belied any such emotion. Under the ever present gaze of Charles, everyone performed efficiently and without reaction to Erasmus' declining physical condition. I repeatedly queried Charles about Erasmus and his medical state, and he always answered that his personal physician examined Erasmus daily and issued instructions at that time. The physician was now with us, ever present, within calling distance of the old man.

As Erasmus was lifted onto the deck, he exclaimed, "Down River to Manhattan, Mr. Jones. We are off to King's College."

"Aye Aye, sir," responded Captain Cleveland. With a wink to me, the eleventh so named Captain Jones of the river launch Elena set off down the Hudson.

On the trip I sat with old Erasmus and we worked continuously on the organization of his federalist essays, continuing to edit and add material that he felt necessary. As we passed Elizabeth, New Jersey, across from New York, Erasmus paused from his work.

"There lays old Elizabethtowne," he said. "It was my good friend Hamilton's first home after arriving from St. Croix. He was an immigrant, you know. Something my conservative friends should remember. We would have no banks, no exchange, no treasury, no government, if it were not for this brilliant, poor, immigrant. Wonderful place, the Caribbean. Wonderful banks."

"You are not conservative?" I teased.

"Of course I am," he snorted back. "I take no part in these liberal Jacobins who would empower the government to protect us from all things, give us all things, and in the end tell us all things. They are a dangerous lot that have in their mind to tell us what to eat, drink, smoke, say, read, and think. Their economics are flawed, their taxes are abusive, and their philosophy is paternal. They are wrong about almost everything."

"But not about immigration?" I said.

"In part, that too, my boy. You see, these leftists have been riding fancy carriages to Paris commune rallies forever, loaded down with the guilt of having been successful instead of applying the capital of that success to the creation of employment and even more capital. They take from capitalists and give to the poor, always taking a cut along the way. You know the richest head of state in the western hemisphere is Fidel Castro? That hypocritical bastard destroyed the highest standard of living in Hamilton's Caribbean, all the while salting away $900 million in banks outside his own country. I know because I own some of the banks."

This response made me pause. First of all, it appeared to have nothing to do with the issue of immigration, upon which we had wandered. Secondly, it was the only direct reference I ever recalled him making to his fabulous wealth.

"What's that to do with liberals and immigration?" I said.

"It's their attitude, my boy. They are pro-immigration because they don't feel we have a sovereign national right to control our borders. And they feel that way because they feel we as a country have no right to do anything. They feel we are always, in everything, ill-intended and wrongfully motivated."

"But the conservatives are wrong too?"

"Obviously," he went on. "We need young workers. We need culturally adaptable, hardworking, family oriented, religious, law-abiding citizens. The types of citizens stable families produce, the types we are no longer producing in sufficient quantities. And we have a whole country of them just south of the Rio."

"So you would open the border?" I asked.

"Not open, my boy, control. Controlled entrance. And I certainly wouldn't let right-wing crackers sit out in the desert on lawn chairs with buffalo rifles. You know they call themselves minutemen? I commanded minutemen, by God, and it infuriates me that they call these people minutemen. A minuteman took a British bayonet in the stomach on Bunker Hill because he had run out of powder. A minuteman staggered under volleys from professional Red Coats on the Lexington green and didn't break ranks. Minutemen bled the snow red at Valley Forge. These bastards take pot shots at unarmed peasants who are risking their lives for the right to mow our lawns and send home $200 a month to their children. Minutemen my ass!" thundered the old man as he spasmed into a cough.

"Easy, old man" I said as the ever watchful physician took a halting step toward the old boy. "We won't solve this problem on a million dollar yacht floating in New York harbor."

"That we won't," he chuckled, as he regained his breath. "But we could lower the pressure. Let the government control the borders as they should, but have entry points where workers can come in. If they work, stay legal, and set up homes, let them be citizens. Then befriend Mexico and help her grow, so there is less reason for her people to come. Send her a Hamilton, so she can banish the scourge of socialism forever. Once that is done, and the crony family companies are owned and traded on a true stock exchange, then she will grow her own middle class. Mexico is our friend, boy. A fine nation and people. And in my heart I know that if her people were not brown, this issue would have a different tone to it", he said.

"In any case, you are right. There is nothing my owning a yacht will do to solve this problem, unless the jobs created by my buying and maintaining it go to immigrants." he continued. "And, for now, your cynical comment about my right to own it will be allowed to pass. Look yonder. There, my friend, is Manhattan. We will land soon, and I will show you where it all began."

With that, Erasmus handed me his work from the night before, no doubt written during another sleepless night. Having anticipated the day's discussion, he had composed his formal response in the form of another essay. He glanced at his attending physician, and retired to his stateroom to change for the landing.

The Lady in the Harbor

❧

My beloved Hamilton was an immigrant, as was my dear friend the Marquis. I warmed myself at Valley Forge with Von Stueben, and I have honored a comrade on Cleveland Heights, above Lake Erie, at the monument to General Pulaski. Even if you hold that servants of our "Glorious Cause" who came from England were not really immigrants, these men still bore that title. And without them we would have been lost.

As I see the Statue of Liberty, perhaps for the last time, I would warn my beloved land that she must remember this fact. American is not a race, nor a color, nor a breed of people. You are an American if, from generation to generation, you are willing to commit yourself to the "Glorious Cause".

Control our borders? If you mean establish a system where there are many Ellis Islands, points of entry where we control the reasonable, orderly, and safe entry of people who wish to work and build a life, then yes, control our borders. If we do not, then any good system of allowing people in who want to work will be overwhelmed with illegal entrants.

Learn the language? Yes. Require a knowledge of history and our laws? Yes. Encourage assimilation? Yes, and again yes, to all of these.

My point is this: Immigration is good for America, and our system should be about making new and good Americans. Those who come to work and are willing to embrace the concept of being American should be naturalized. This debate should not be about how to keep people out. It should be about the best way to let the best people in. If people that are already here are doing everything we would ask of a person who we would let in, then let them stay. If a person will do all those things we would have them do, then let them in. We need these people, these workers, these potential Americans. It is in our best interest, if we do it right, to welcome them.

If we, however, out of nationalism, misplaced protectionism, racism, or simple fear, fail to act rightly even when it is in our own economic interest to do so, then, my friends, we must close the border and build a military wall.

In doing so we would create a new Eastern Europe in South America, and create enemies where we now have friends. Fences, barbed wire, brick walls, soldiers, checkpoints—are these not the tools of tyrants? How do these things serve the cause of freedom, the "Glorious Cause" to which Hamilton, Pulaski, and Lafayette flocked?

These men, their spirits, they watch us still. I drift now in New York harbor. The gaze of the Lady holding her torch is upon me. Towering above me, she wonders, what will we do?

We have interests, concerns—legitimate ones—yet we are still the hope of the world. Will we remain so? She watches, and she wonders.

Tacitus

Chapter Twenty
King's College

We landed at a private slip at the yacht club on the southern tip of Manhattan Island, and I was no longer surprised to be met by a myriad of servants, porters, drivers, and assistants. They all knew Charles, and reacted sharply and efficiently to his instructions. All seemed aware of Erasmus' declining health, yet none made mention. He showed respect in his demeanor, even as they had to help him off the launch. And this respect was returned to him ten fold.

It is said that when Vanderbilt constructed his beautiful Biltmore mansion, he kept 2500 men working for nearly five years. From the Gilded Age to the New Deal, titans like Milton, Vanderbilt, Rockefeller, Morgan, and Ford felt putting men to work was a good, ethical, even charitable use of their wealth. This was a belief if even employing men in the providing for their own excess. Erasmus took pride in the employment of these people who served him. He often expressed shock and anger at those who demeaned service jobs, and hotly maintained that there is dignity in all work. It was a vestige of his time. And never once did I see anyone in that capacity display anything but love for the old man.

Upon arrival, I expected a tour of the magnificent Columbia University. This was the school where Milton and Hamilton were classmates, and from which they graduated.

It was, as Erasmus said, "where it all began". I naturally thought we would head to Morningstar Heights, see the famous Butler Library, and pay homage at the statue of Columbia's most famous alumnus, the great Alexander Hamilton. All of this we eventually did. But first, ignoring all the famous statutes and buildings, we went to lower Broadway, and found the site of the Old Trinity Church.

"Here," Erasmus said. "Here, in the old church school, is where King's College began. They started teaching here in 1754 with a charter from King George. The old rascal knew Princeton was turning out patriots and rabble-rousers by the dozen, and he wanted a Tory counter balance.

"My good friend Hamilton had emigrated from St. Croix, and spent eight months at Elizabethtown Academy preparing himself for entrance to one of our nine colonial colleges. His sponsors pushed Princeton, and he would have gone there had they accepted his bold demand that he be allowed to progress through the grades as quickly as his abilities would allow. But they did not, and in the fall of 1773 he ended up here with me, studying under that old Tory, Dr. Cooper.

"We did well here, and we were close enough to the park for Alexander and me to begin mixing with the local "liberty boys." We started giving speeches in City Hall Park, and by the time the struggle began, we were leaders of a student militia unit.

We studied the Enlightenment's Locke and Hume, and we learned Blackstone's common law. It was not the best school in the colonies, but we were there at a good time. We left prepared. We gave up our semi-monarchist thoughts here, and became patriots.

"You know, where we landed today there was located a battery of patriot guns. Alexander and I led our unit there and saved them from confiscation. We took fire from a British ship in the harbor. We saved seven of the guns by dragging them to the city commons, and buried two more here at the campus. To my knowledge, those two fire-spitting nine-pounders are still here, under the Broadway sidewalk," Erasmus beamed.

That evening we were taken by a private car to Central Park, and were driven to a beautiful building where Erasmus owned several sets of apartments. Beda and I had our own suite. "I have business in the city, and must again visit my doctor," Erasmus said. "The driver is at your disposal. Enjoy yourselves, for in two days we will head north."

I answered a knock at the door of our room later that night, and it was Charles. "Master Milton has asked me to deliver this to you. It is from our friend Tacitus."

"So you know of Tacitus? I suspected as much" I replied.

"I have known of him, and of your efforts, for quite some time. I am very grateful to you sir, for this kindness you are showing Mr. Milton" he said. "He has served the "Cause" with great distinction, and his omission from our history is an injustice."

"I need to know, Charles, if you are aware of his disorder?" I asked.

"There is you, your family, the physician, and myself, sir. And until his death, this must remain so. After that, you are released from all pledges but one. He has trusted you to follow his instructions exactly upon his demise, as concerns his personal correspondence. These instructions are included with the last essay. It would be expected that once you have read it, you will destroy that portion of the letter."

I read the letter, and was for a moment dumbfounded at what was being asked of me. But I had given my word. Then I read the final Tacitus essay, and realized that there was indeed nothing that I would not do for this old man.

Founding Father

There is, to this day, debate as to the authorship of the Federalist Papers. I can attest, as I was there, that the spirit, the soul, and most of the text were Hamilton's. His production I can describe only as prolific. In my efforts as his assistant, I edited, embellished, and in some ways completed his words. But they were his.

Madison and Jay were contributors, but more so was I. In my last conversation with my beloved Hamilton, on July 9, 1804, I went to talk him away from that insidious episode with the faux patriot Burr. He refused to dismiss it, and I became angry.

"You know, this is so like you," I scolded. "We lead a band of patriots up the redoubt walls of Yorktown. I am with you step for step, yet you receive the glory. Together we drag this republic kicking and screaming toward a constitution, and I do not get to sign it. Our federalist efforts are published, with you as the author, and my name is nowhere to be seen. We start the bank and the stock exchange. You invent our government from scratch, and I am with you at every turn. Now I, whose place in history is totally tied to yours, am to be left in obscurity while you risk all to achieve honor in a duel with an honorless man. It is not fair, Alexander, that you should leave it so between us. If you die and leave this injustice to me unresolved, I will not rest until it is corrected."

"You make a bold claim, sir. I admit, however, that you are right. I have done you an injustice. My pride and desire for recognition have led me to harm the one most responsible for my own success. Forgive me dear friend" he replied to me. "After I settle this matter with Burr, I will address our efforts together in a written history. The record will be set straight. I promise that before your body dies, your place among the Founders will be secure. You have been a brother to me since our time together at King's College. I thank you Erasmus, you have been always true to the "Cause."

This was our last conversation. He refused to withdraw from the duel, and I refused to be his second. I drove the coach to the duel, but would not stand the field with him. By the time we reached his house after his being shot, he was unconscious. He died on July 12, 1804. It was on that day that my aging ceased.

As is true of so many of his words, they could have been addressed not just to the hearer, but to the nation throughout the ages. "Be always true to the "Cause."

What does this phrase mean to us? In my final essay, I think I can say that it means this:

Hold true to the truth of the "Glorious Cause", and don't disparage it because the deliverers of it, the Founders, were not perfect men.

Because Jefferson was not perfect does not mean that he was not right. Our fundamental liberties do not need to be proven. They are self-evident. We are endowed by our Creator with the right to govern our own lives, to speak our minds and worship our God, and to keep and better our property. These rights accrue not to animals, not to soil or stone, nor to governments or principalities. They accrue only to humanity, all humanity, and they are what make us human.

While our beloved General Washington was not perfect, he was indeed right in saying that we must not exclude God from our public life. Our government is not seen today as good, or competent, or just, because it has removed divine endowment as its claim to goodness. It is divine endowment that turned kings into despots, but it is that same endowment that makes liberty eternal. It must be restored.

The "Glorious Cause" that founded America should always be what America is. Democracy should be worshipped. It is worthy of praise. It should be spread when it is prudent and possible to do so, for its basis, liberty, is universal.

My long life is nearly over. I have been blessed to live to see my beloved land grow and prosper. I am optimistic about its future, but it is time to give it over to you, the people of that future.

As I depart, I pray the blessings of liberty perpetually for you. I go now to the banquet to which I aspire. You have read my papers and judged me worthy. There I will find Washington, Adams, Jefferson, Morris, Madison, Jay, Franklin, and the rest. I will raise a glass with them, and I will share a toast with the inventor of our government, my friend, my Hamilton. I was there at the beginning, and I belong there now. For, alas, I am a Founding Father.

Tacitus

Chapter Twenty-One
Rest

After such a dire essay, I despaired of my old friend's health, and, as we all tend to do with loved ones, I occupied my mind with ways to prolong his life. I met with his doctor the next morning, who described Erasmus' health as "remarkable for a man his age, but certainly not well."

"Besides," he said, "his course of treatment he himself has laid out quite specifically, and I am forbidden to alter or discuss it."

Erasmus, as always, responded well to the two days of rest while Beda and I utilized his driver to tour the history of his life in New York. By week's end, we were heading north on I-95 for the six hour drive to Maine.

Erasmus' private caravan stopped briefly at Portland's jet port to pick up my oldest son Tim and his wife Katie.

Tim was a Colby alumnus and wanted to join us for the trip to his alma mater, so Erasmus flew them from Dayton, Ohio, to Portland, Maine. It was my oldest son who understood best Erasmus' need to venture back to this serene place in time of stress or tragedy. He too knew the peace of this place, and shared a love for it. To the best of my knowledge they met only briefly at Colby, although Erasmus was indeed well known there.

Tim attended a speech given by Erasmus once, and questioned him afterward. He racked his mind trying to decide or remember if he had mentioned me, Ohio, or anything that might have connected myself to the old man. But there was nothing. I still wonder often if it was this spiritual bridge, provided by my son and my friend and their mutual love for Colby, which Erasmus crossed to find his way to me.

From Portland it was a seventy minute drive to the village of Waterville, up Mayflower Hill, and to the most beautiful campus in North America, Colby College.

Erasmus, as you know, was a part of a small group of businessmen and clergy who had founded Colby in 1813, known then as The Literary and Theological Institution of Maine. Erasmus had spent time in Waterville, seeking lumber for his fledgling shipbuilding and trade business, and he had fallen in love with the place. In 1804 he had sought refuge in Waterville from a deep depression brought on by the loss of his friend Hamilton. He had returned often, to grieve for his Elena, to hear Emerson, to mourn Lovejoy and Shaw. Many times in his life, it was his sanctuary. For here he could find, in the extraordinary beauty of this place, a peace of mind that eluded him everywhere else. I found it both saddening and fitting, then, that he had returned here to die.

The first evening here he had a private dinner with the president of the college at his home, and it seems Erasmus had a guest suite there in which he always was accommodated. The next day he spent the morning walking the campus with Tim, educating him on the unique and glorious history of Colby, from it's religious beginnings to its proud abolitionism and participation in the civil rights movement, to its being the first New England men's college to admit women, to the odd fact of it being the site of the first ever intercollegiate women's hockey match. Erasmus knew everything about this school, and it was obvious that he loved it so.

That evening, Erasmus, with the aid of his recently acquired portable oxygen bottle, gave a special lecture to the economics and history students on the American financial system during the revolutionary period. Billed as "New England's preeminent re-enactor of the revolutionary period," he appeared in his original, astonishing continental officer's uniform. He was magnificent. For two hours he regaled the students and faculty with amazing tales of his and Hamilton's escapades. From the staff rooms of Washington's army, to Saratoga and Yorktown, to the secret shenanigans employed by Hamilton to save the new nation's credit. He told it all, and the audience, as always, was enthralled.

When done, he politely declined a reception at the president's home, and asked me to walk with him. We went out alone on the steps of the beautiful library, and up the hill to the Lorimer chapel.

Walking through the stunning Maine evening under an incredible starlit sky, he told me again of the young Elijah Lovejoy, martyr to the abolitionist cause. He spoke tearfully again of his "Colby Boys," who had volunteered to fight and die in the "war to free the slaves." He beamed with pride over this place, and its peace had again returned to him.

Still in his uniform, he took me inside the chapel, and we sat in the front pew. For a final time, I was blessed to have time alone with this beloved old man, and listen to his wisdom, his stories, and his voice.

"You have published my essays as you promised, my boy. I know the little Lafayette paper doesn't seem like much to you, but it was to me. A firm in Boston has taken measures to publish them more broadly, and my little town and its newspaper will greatly benefit. As for you, you have been my savior. Do not fret over your role in my aging. You and your lovely family were finally my family as it should have been. I will not lose you, nor your wife, nor will I see my little Matty age and die. Finally, those I love will mourn for me. It is as it should be. For restoring my family, and for your friendship and your love, I thank you."

Removing a string of beads from his vest that I knew to be Elena's rosary, he said, "Now if I could have a moment, I would like to pray."

Being able to compose myself no longer, and not wanting to have him see me weep, I turned to leave the chapel. As I reached the door, he spoke to me once more without ever turning from his prayers: "You know, my boy, I speak often of the Founders. They were my friends. I want you to know that I hold you also in such esteem as these, my comrades. Oh, my boy, if you had been there. Such men, such men. And I think had you been there, you would have been with us, loyal to the 'Cause'. All times are, in their own way, great times, you know. And there is no time that does not have need of honorable men. Stay true to the "Cause" boy, stay true to our Glorious Cause."

I left the chapel, and on the steps stood the ever-present doctor. He politely ignored my tears, nodded a good evening, and went inside. There he found Colonel Erasmus Milton, hero of the Revolution and Founding Father, dressed as he should be in full uniform, kneeling at the altar in Lorimer Chapel, Colby College, Waterville, Maine. He had died still keeping his promise to his Elena, clutching her rosary, saying his prayers, being as good a Catholic as a New England Presbyterian could be. And he had found rest.

Epilogue

We learned of Erasmus' death at our hotel the next morning. Erasmus, being who he was, he had prearranged everything. His body was transported back to his Hudson River estate. He was laid to rest in his colonial officer's uniform, with military honors, beside Elena. The presidents from Columbia, Colby, and Ohio Northern attended, as did military and political dignitaries of every sort. His entire staff wept with grief.

The knowledge of my relationship with him was more well-known than I thought. Senator John McCain introduced himself. Noting that his family could trace their military history on his mother's side all the way back to General Washington, he wanted to thank me for arranging for him to receive originals of military correspondence bearing his ancestor's signature. "Do you have any idea how he came to be in possession of such documents?" the Senator ask. "They are magnificent."

"I do not, sir," I replied. "But you must know that Mr. Milton had an amazing life, and nothing I find out now will surprise me."

The Historical Society of Mount Vernon sent a representative to thank us for artifacts long thought lost.

The Navel Academy sent a note of thanks for the donation of a sword belonging to John Paul Jones, one thought lost with the sinking of the Bohème Richard. On the base of its blade was etched "To Milton, with thanks, J.P. Jones."

Such unimaginable and impossible events became commonplace that day, and by evening everyone had a full understanding of the treasure we had lost in Erasmus' passing.

We learned soon after the funeral that our vehicle, having been stranded in Buffalo nearly a month before, had been returned to my home in Ohio. Charles had given me an exact itinerary for post funeral, and we were soon flown home.

At the appointed time and day in early December, I made the short drive to Lafayette, Ohio, to Erasmus' last home. Waiting for me there, equally obedient to the old man's strict schedule, were historians from Colby and Columbia. I had been instructed by Charles to act for Ohio Northern. Vans from each school had also arrived, and a large number of labeled trunks of artifacts and papers, coded by school, were loaded onto each. As the other two gentlemen left, they thanked me for "my uncle's generosity." They noted he had given millions of dollars at his death to each school, as well as the priceless artifacts. I confirmed his generosity, and thanked them for their kindness to him on his visits.

Everyone had now gone, and I was left alone at the house with my memories of the old patriot. So many times I had spent fascinating days in this old house, living through Erasmus the wonderful history of his life, and the life of our nation. This final day was ending, but I had one more fascinating and painful instruction to carry out. For one final time, I opened the door to the stair case which led up to the place where Erasmus' possessions had first proven to me the truth of his outlandish claims.

As I reached the top of the stairs, I saw that the attic, always full of all the things of Erasmus' life, was now empty. It was swept clean and contained nothing, save a large chest in the middle of the room, a lamp, a small desk and chair, a large bronze waste paper container, and, on a hanger, a colonial uniform and sword. On the uniform was a note in familiar hand, which read simply "For Master Matthew, Love, Papa Milton."

I instantly recognized the chest. It was the one item I was never allowed to breach, as it had always been locked. It was labeled "personal correspondence", and the old pad lock that has always kept the chest safely out of the reach of any prying eyes was now gone.

Obeying my instructions, I opened the trunk and began to read. These letters were amazing. Love letters to Elena, personal exchanges with Washington, Hamilton, Govneur Morris, and all the others. Notes begging Hamilton to make apologies and not proceed with the duel.

Caring and loving letters between Elisa Hamilton and the Miltons all throughout Mrs. Hamilton's fifty years of widowhood. And finally, heart breaking correspondence between an ever young Erasmus and his aging beloved Elena. I read for hours, never stopping. I laughed, I was enthralled, I wept uncontrollably, I lived with Erasmus his incredible blessing and curse of his "rather odd tendency to not age at a normal rate."

I finally understood, and even endured with him his glory, his pain, and his grief. To have endured it, and stayed true to his "Glorious Cause" through the changes of time was a truly amazing feat.

After completing each letter, I dutifully dropped it in the bronze tub beside the desk. When the case was empty, except for a final envelope, I dropped in a match and burned the final literary remains of my friend Erasmus Milton. These letters, in his hand, were the proof that he had lived so long, and done so much. They were my proof that he was indeed here, and that I had known him. And now they were gone.

Having kept my last and most difficult promise, I opened the last envelope. I had been instructed that I would find it at the bottom of the chest, and that it would be addressed to me. I smiled when I saw the title written in Erasmus' hand on the outside of the envelope. Here is what it said:

Letter to an Ohio Gentleman

I am truly sorry, sir, to have had to ask you to burn my personal papers. They are your proof of who I really was, and now they are gone. But the information in them was personal, and I had no permission to disclose it. There are items there, as you now know, that would have embarrassed the ancestors of my closest friends. Historians would have found some items unbelievable and outlandish and called you a fraud. Revisionist historians, not willing to accrue human weakness and normalcy onto the founding brotherhood, would have used these letters to tarnish our "Glorious Cause".

I could trust no one but you to complete this final task. In keeping your word to publish my life's work in your tiny paper, you have proven to me that you would indeed keep your promises. And it was this final promise, above all, that I needed you to keep.

You scolded me once for writing under a pseudonym, and I told you that some day you would stumble across his works, see a quote, and understand. Allow me, my good friend, to save you the time of that search. Here is the quote, addressing what was, other than my years with Elena, the happiest time of my life. When you read it, you will indeed understand my choice.

"I have reserved as an employment of my old age, should I live long enough, to write of things that you may find fruitful and helpful to the Empire. For I am enjoying now the rarest and happiest of times, when we may think what we please, and express what we think..."

Tacitus, *The Annals and the Histories*
Written At Rome, 90 AD

Rest assured, when you come to the place I am now, I shall introduce you to my lovely Elena, and we will raise a glass with my founding friends. I will introduce you as my dear friend, who was always true to our "Glorious Cause."

Forever your friend,

Erasmus Milton

Acknowledgements

While *Founding Father* is a novel, I have tried to be as accurate as my recollections would allow as concerns historical facts. I have read extensively in history, and much of the historical material is based on those readings.

To the extent I gleaned facts or quotes from my history books, here are the credits:

Alexander Hamilton
By Ron Chernow"
The Penguin Press 2004

Faith of my Fathers
By John McCain
Random House 1999

Forged in Battle
By Joseph T. Glatthaar
Free Press 1990

Washington
By James Thomas Flexner
Little, Brown & Co. 1974

A More Perfect Union
By William Peters
Crown Publishers 1987

John Paul Jones
By Evan Thomas
Simon & Schuster 2003

Slavery and the Making of America
By James and Lois Horton
Oxford University Press 2005

General and Madame de Lafayette
By Jason Lane
Taylor Trade Publishing 2003

Great Books
"Tacitus"
Britannica 1994

The American Reader
Edited by Diane Ravitch
Harper Collins 1990

The First American
By H. W. Brands
Doubleday 2000

Printed in the United States
65434LVS00004B/394-420